MOON BLOOD

THE FIRST BLOOD SON SERIES

BOOK 5

CAROL MCKIBBEN

www.trollriverpub.com

Moon Blood
The First Blood Son Book 5
Copyright © 2019 Carol McKibben
ISBN: 978-1-946454-74-4
Editor: Ravi Banthia
Cover Design: Kritzel Kunst

Other books by Carol McKibben:

<u>The Snow Blood series:</u>

Snow Blood: Season 1

Snow Blood Season 2

Snow Blood: Season 3

Snow Blood: Season 4

Snow Blood: Season 5

Kane:

The First Blood Son (prequel of the Snow Blood series)

<u>The First Blood Son series:</u>

Moon Blood: The First Blood Son series (Book 1)

Moon Blood: The First Blood Son series (Book 2)

Moon Blood: The First Blood Son series (Book 3)

Moon Blood: The First Blood Son series (Book 4)

<u>The Silver Blood Knight series:</u>

REIGN: The Assault of Lucifer Morningstar

They were unique among their kind.

Ancients were the firstborn of the originals. They didn't seek out destruction or evil. It sought them, challenged them, and tried to possess them.

Kane de Medici is the powerful first blood son of Brogio, the original vampire. Devoted to learning, he has chosen a life of knowledge and experimentation. After centuries of war and battle, he longs for peace and fulfillment with those he loves.

Moon, Kane's hybrid-wolf progeny, is loyal to him above all, while Enzo, her magical spirit wolf, is devoted to her protection.

Zandra Moretti is the firstborn of King Lycaon, the original werewolf. She and her ten brothers are hybrid vampire Lycans committed to not harming innocents and to fighting for what is right. Kane is the love of Zandra's existence, and with him, she and her brothers will give their lives to fight against the evil that endlessly seeks to capture or destroy him.

Anointed as God's chosen warriors, they are pitted against Satan and all manner of evil from their past. Giving their all to protect each other and humanity, the de Medici vampires must face the ultimate test of their strength, skills, and intelligence. Underneath it all, love and loyalty are the keys to victory with Moon and Enzo showing them the way.

The ultimate clash of Good against Evil plays out in *Moon Blood Book 5*, the culmination of the First Blood Son Series.

CONTENTS

DEDICATION

For Donald Weller because of all his love and support. This book was written while staying on his ranch, and it was his generosity that gave me the time to do it. And to Rett, Lauren, Diesel, and Slater for loving me from afar.

For Stephanie, who always makes me better.

For Mark for putting up with my "do not disturb me" moments.

For all those mornings on the front porch with Thor, Charlie, Emma, MeMe and Ty. You slowed the writing process but made my life better.

And for my readers. You have encouraged me and shared your thoughts of this series with me. Without you, I could get discouraged.

SNOW BLOOD/MOON BLOOD SERIES CAST OF CHARACTERS

Brogio (Ambrogio) – The first vampire

Snow Blood – Brogio's white husky vampire dog and constant companion

Kane de Medici – Brogio's first blood (vampire) son

Selene – Moon goddess and love of Brogio's existence

Nova – Enemy then mate to Snow Blood

Tommy – Boy master to Snow Blood when he was just a dog

Leander – Vampire coven leader and friend to Brogio; the second blood son of Brogio

Ian – Vampire coven leader, former wine worker for Brogio and husband to Leslie

Leslie – Vampire coven leader, former wine worker for Brogio and wife to Ian

Marco – Vampire coven leader, former soldier, and Kane's cousin and progeny

Mia – Vampire coven leader and previous girlfriend of Kane's

Joseph – Vampire coven leader and former pickpocket

Alexander – Vampire coven leader and former officer in the pope's army

Scrawny – Snow Blood's wolf progeny and second-in-command

Chase – Snow Blood's progeny and fastest member of his coven

Gaspar – Snow Blood's progeny and guardian member of his coven

Joker – Snow Blood's progeny and playful member of his coven

Thor – Snow Blood's progeny and warrior member of his coven

Fergus – Snow Blood's progeny and wise member of his coven

Adam – Brogio and Selene's human son

Moon Blood – Kane's vampire hybrid wolf progeny, constant companion, and biological daughter of Snow Blood and Nova

Zandra Moretti – Firstborn of the original werewolf and Kane's love interest whom he turned hybrid vampire Lycan

James – Servant to Kane and later Zandra's hybrid vampire Lycan progeny

Zandra's brothers – Zeb, Zachary, Zale, Zander, Zeno, Zindel, Zane, Zylon, Zohar, Zoltan – all original werewolf descendants turned hybrid vampire Lycans by Kane

Thomas and the kresniks – Vampire hunters sent to destroy Brogio and his family

Mia – A kresnik and wife of Thomas

Artemis – Goddess of the forests, the hunt, and the moon; arch enemy to Brogio

Apollo – God of the sun and twin brother to Artemis, also arch enemy to Brogio

Hades – God of the Underworld and keeper of all vampire souls

Zeus – Master of the gods and god of thunder

Poseidon – God of the oceans

Seth – White witch, fallen angel, and restored angel friend to Kane

Mathias – Black-winged Friesian horse angel and companion to Seth

Michael – Archangel

Gabriel – Archangel

Raphael – Archangel

Hecate – Goddess of the witches and enemy to the vampires

Glenna – White witch friend to Seth

Emma – Seth's human love and the reason he fell from grace

Corso – Hunter with magical powers sent to destroy Brogio

Trivia – Identical in appearance to Emma, she pursues Seth

Persephone – Wife of Hades and friend to Hecate and Selene

Dina – Hades' werewolf spy

Kronos – Titan

Elon Musk – Kane's employer

Leonardo da Vinci – The great artist/inventor to whom Kane apprenticed as a human

Novette, Moonlight, Tommy, Scrawny, Seth, and Mathias – Snow Blood and Nova's hybrid pups

Natalia – Corporate spy and enemy of Kane and Moon Blood

Topher Bruns – CEO of United Rockets and an enemy to Kane

Detectives Winchester and Samson – LAPD officers investigating Kane

Bernice – Elon Musk's assistant

Alemain – Wolf pack leader that attack's Snow Blood's pack

Griffin – Leader of the berserkers or flesh eaters

King Lycaon – The first werewolf and sire to Zandra and her brothers

Agnar – A second leader of the berserkers

Ingolf – Son of Agnar

Eric – Third berserker leader

Lilith – The original succubus and enemy to Kane, Moon, and their family

Samil – Satan in wolf form

Matteo Ricci – Remaining berserker leader

Diego and Paolo Ricci – Matteo's brothers

Magnum – Shadowhunter who aids Kane and Moon

Jubal – Another Shadowhunter

Enzo – Spirit wolf to Moon Blood

Zombies and skeleton fighters – Vampire enemies

Sam Black – Emissary from Elon Musk

Satan/Lucifer Morningstar – Enemy of Kane and his family

Noble – Servant to Kane

Calliope – Prostitute that Kane mistakenly turns into a vampire ripper

SNOW BLOOD FAMILY TREE

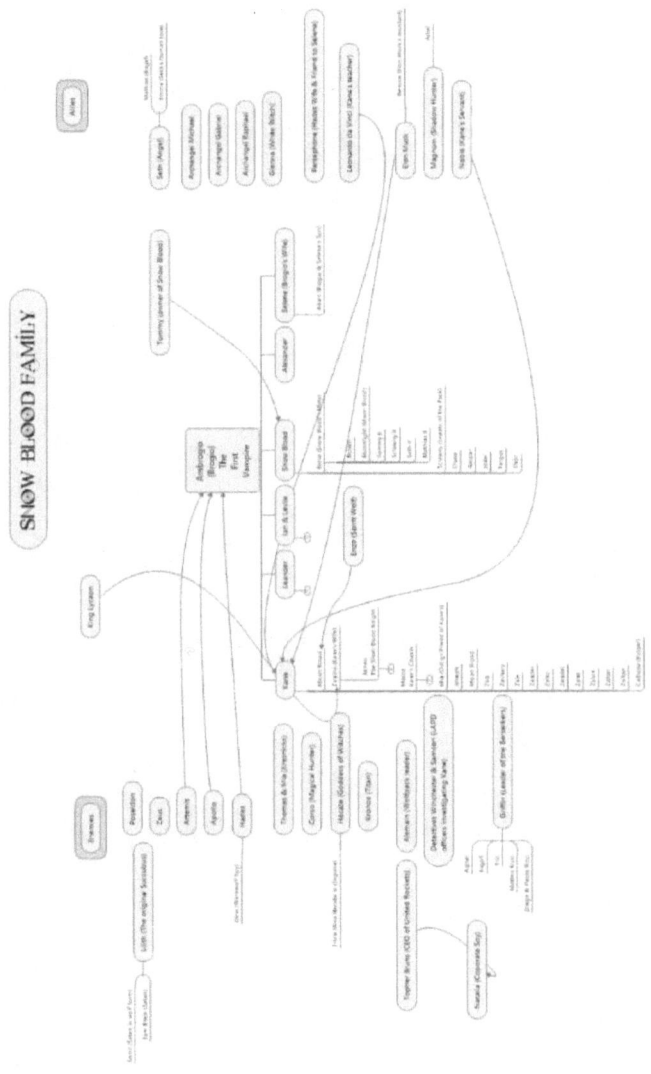

For a larger version, go to:
http://www.carolmckibben.com/snowbloodfamilytree.html

EPISODE ONE

THE COMING

Enzo's shaggy black fur shimmered in the Tuscany moonlight. His golden eyes transfixed on nothing. His body stood frozen in place. I knew the signs. My spirit-turned-corporeal wolf was experiencing another vision.

The forest around us just outside my master Kane's Italian wine estate was silent save the laughing voices of Zandra, her brothers, and James, her newly turned hybrid vampire Lycan, as they hunted for prey in the far distance. They had no need to be quiet as their vampire speed allowed them to take down the fastest prey. Through my preternatural connection to Kane, I alerted to my sire taking down a large bull moose and sating his thirst at the beast's jugular. I longed to have a taste.

Instead, I padded to Enzo and pressed against him until his eyes focused and he shook his head. I sat back on my haunches as he gazed into my eyes.

We will have little rest. The worst approaches.

His warning shook me to the core. I twisted my head at the one I loved only second to Kane and wondered, *What could be worse than what we have experienced? Enemy werewolves, flesh eaters, shifters, and zombies have attacked us repeatedly. Lilith, the original succubus, has tried to control us. Satan has tried to destroy us. Prior to ever meeting you, human greed captured and tried to use us.*

Before he could telepathically respond, we both lifted our noses to the air and took in the stench of danger lurking around us.

An arrow whizzed past my right ear. A sharp sting and the whiff of deadly silver alerted me as a chunk of my furry white ear sailed through the air.

Enzo whirled and placed his backside to mine. We circled as some twenty men dressed in brown leather pants and boots surrounded us. They carried axes, crossbows, and swords. Their faces and bodies reeked of hate.

My injured ear stung. The insidious burn of it seeped inward from the minor cut. Liquid fire ran down the rest of my injured appendage numbing everything it touched. I feared silver poison but ignored it and sprang just missing the sharp side of an axe intended for me. I went for the hunter's weapon-wielding arm and bit down.

The man screamed, convulsed, and foamed at the mouth. He died before he hit the ground.

Behind me, I heard Enzo tear into several others. Skin and cloth ripped. Screams of humans being devoured rang through the air. The spirit wolf's throaty growls and gnashing teeth mingled with their cries.

A few of the enemy backed off momentarily in surprise at Enzo's ferocity and their comrade's death from my one bite. They must not have known that I had inherited my biological father Snow Blood's deadly bite. I took off to my right, grabbed the extended arm of one man, and ripped it from his shoulder. He shuddered and fell face first into the budding spring ground cover. I whirled and this time bit into the leg nearest me. Knowing I had killed again, I moved on and sprang, tearing out the throat of a third victim.

The screams of those Enzo attacked were short-lived. His powerful jaws ripped throat after throat. Dead bodies littered the forest ground. The smell of their blood incited me. The bloodlust within me overpowered my senses.

I leapt for another would-be victim but was taken down by a silver arrow to my spine. The pain shot through every nerve ending, and the deadly metal surged through my core paralyzing me. Four more attackers surrounded me and began to slash and hack at me with both swords and axes. A blade bit deeply into my shoulder. I yelped in agony. The pain became intolerable.

Enzo instantly jumped them and became a killing machine. Body parts flew in the air. A head rolled next to me. The man's blank, dead eyes stared at me. An arm plopped down just next to the head. A headless torso took flight and smashed against an oak tree.

I struggled to stand as another blow landed on me from behind, taking my hind legs out from under me. I whirled and took off the offending hand with one bite. The soft appendage still wiggled. My body began to morph into my inner demon, but blood poured from me. I fought to keep my eyes open and was sinking fast. I felt my life slipping away.

As another attacker bent to slice my throat, I sprang with all my remaining strength and tore out his. With nothing left, I slid toward the earth. As the world went dark, I heard Kane's voice. *Hold on, girl. We're here.*

∞

My consciousness swam up to the surface. Something pulled at me to fall back into the peaceful darkness, but I resisted and opened my eyes to blurry figures. I blinked, and my eyes focused. Kane and Enzo hovered over me.

Kane's gentle hand stroked my forehead and comforted me as he yanked the silver arrow from my spine. His hand smoldered from the metal. He flung it away from us and shook out his hand as if to ward off the pain of it.

Lie still, my girl. Let my blood heal your injuries. Blood trickled down my throat. He held his slashed wrist over my mouth, and I licked at it with all my strength.

Enzo licked my injured shoulder. Then he went to work on the hole the arrow had left at the base of my spine and my injured leg. His rough tongue brought me comfort, and I felt my strength returning.

I turned my head in embarrassment at being laid low by our attackers.

My spirit wolf nudged my head with his nose. *You fought valiantly. You took out six of them before you were surrounded by a group of them. Do not feel shame.*

I tried to hide my disappointment in myself and looked around.

Zandra sat nearby. Black tears streaked down her face from her golden eyes. Her thoughts surged into my brain and inserted her will on me. *Heal, heal, Moon.*

Her words filled my brain.

Her brothers and James went around hacking up the bodies of our attackers into small pieces. Since no heads remained attached to bodies, they used their long swords to slice torsos in half and then quarters and chop up arms and legs. Loose heads were placed on tree stumps and cut into four pieces. The surroundings reeked of death. Blood saturated the forest ground. The sight of it was gruesome even to me.

Why are they chopping up the slain bodies? I struggled to get up, but Kane's firm hand pushed me back down.

Out of spite. Kane smirked at me and continued communicating with me in our preferred method of using telepathy. *No one harms our beloved girl and gets away with it.*

As I stayed still to heal as my master had commanded, I watched James and Zandra's brothers. Love filled my heart when I was with them.

James had been Kane's loyal servant for years. He had first belonged to Brogio, Kane's sire, who passed him along to my master. Before turning, he had been a gray, unnoticeable man who lived in the shadows. The only thing he had ever wanted in this world was to be one of us. Finally, because of James' undying service, Kane had asked Zandra to turn him so that James could be a hybrid vampire Lycan and daywalker as she and her brothers were. James could better serve all of us as one who could live in the sun. Over time, James and I had become good friends. Now, as kindred, he was anything but unnoticeable. His gray hair had gone white. His gray eyes had become a deeper, brilliant shade of slate and pierced through to my soul when he looked my way. Before the transformation he wore all-black suits that remained impeccable even when I splashed into the pool while he cleared the filters. He now dressed in white or silver. Dirt never penetrated his suits. Not even now as he hacked at the dead bodies, blood splatters refused to fly his way. Had to be magic. Or perhaps his clothing was impervious to dirt like my long white hair?

Zandra's brothers had proven their loyalty beyond a doubt. Individually, they were monster sized. Together, they dwarfed everything around them. Each had to be as tall or taller than my sire, who was six foot five. Their broad shoulders led down to beefy, hairy arms. Each had long dark hair in varying shades of brown or black. Their olive skin and golden eyes matched those of their sister, Zandra.

I watched them as they worked chopping bodies. Zeb, the oldest, sliced off an arm in anger. He looked back at me briefly and winked. Then his eyes fell on his sister and melted with love and devotion.

Zachary, the second oldest brother, appeared to grow larger as he tossed a head playfully at the rugged but charming Zale who grinned and gave his brother a full salaam greeting. He placed his hand in the center of his chest over the heart, palm to chest, then moved it upward to touch his forehead, then rotated the palm out and up slightly above his head in a sweeping motion.

Zachary waved his brother off and focused on his work at hand.

Zander, the shy one, worked quietly and stacked body parts neatly as he cut them off.

Zeno, Zindel, and Zane smirked and joked as they worked.

Zeno called to them in his mind. *What do you call a tower made of body parts?*

Zane laughed out loud and responded. *Body building. What else!*

Zindel put his axe down and scratched his chin. *That's lame! I've got a better one. What human body part is long, hard, bendable, and contains the letters p,e,n,i,s?*

Zeno and Zane stopped quartering a torso together and stared at each other.

Zindel threw back his head and roared laughing. *Your SPINE, stupids!* He puffed out his chest at besting his brothers.

Zeno and Zane rolled their eyes, stood tall, and went back to work.

The three proud brothers smiled with satisfaction as they worked, as always, together.

Zohar looked over and gave me a nonchalant and carefree nod. His inner spirit embraced freedom and fun.

Zoltan's sensitive eyes were filled with concern as he met mine. I had to admit he was my favorite, and we had developed an instant connection.

Zylon scowled as he pulled apart limbs with his bare hands. Second to Zeb, he terrified me at times. If I didn't have the venom to kill in an instant, I wouldn't want to do battle with any of them, but particularly Zylon.

Enzo shook me from my thoughts as he took a last lick and dashed to a dissected body, which he began to devour.

No need for that, Kane called to the spirit wolf. *Kresniks don't reanimate.*

Enzo spat out a mouthful and shot back to my master, *Good thing. They taste terrible.*

Kane threw back his head and laughed out loud, his long dark hair touching his waist when he did. Fixing his dark-brown eyes on me, he ran his hand over my shoulder. *You are healing well. You can sit up now that you have functioning hind legs again.*

I struggled until I got my hind under me and then sat back on my haunches. *Kresniks?*

Vampire hunters, Moon. Sworn enemies. My sire Brogio killed Thomas, their leader, some years ago. His wife Mia, too, and most of his kind at the time.

I moved my paws from side to side and then tested my ability to stand. *Then, why would they attack us now?* I turned to Enzo. *Is this the "worst" you predicted? That you saw in your vision?*

Kane whirled toward Enzo. *What did you see? Damn! Will these attacks never stop?*

I saw…

Before Enzo could answer, the unfurling of wings startled us all. A blinding light covered the entire area in front of us. White wings spread at least six feet to either side of a slowly emerging figure. Streaming from above and landing to the figure's side, another bright light contained a dark figure with a wingspan that equaled those of its companion. Seth, Kane's long-time angel friend, and Mathias, his black Friesian companion, emerged from the light and floated toward us.

Kane and Zandra stood, and the hybrid vampire Lycan's brothers and James drew closer to us.

Kane walked with an extended hand as Seth neared. When their fingertips touched, a white light enveloped the two figures. The light magnified the beauty of each. Merely calling Seth handsome would be an injustice. *Beautiful* was the correct word. As tall as my master, he stood with long pale-blond hair flowing over broad shoulders. Clothed in a white robe, Seth spread his wings briefly as he took my master's outstretched hand. The angel's piercing blue eyes sparkled in his fair-skinned, perfect face. He was a mirror in white to Kane's dark hair and eyes and pale skin. Both had strong jaws and noses. Today, my master was dressed in all black. As he had taken over the reins of vampire leadership of all kindred from his now-human sire, Brogio, he had grown away from the dandy clothing he had once loved. It was as if the weight of leadership had sobered the first blood son in all ways. But it hadn't dampened his magnetic appearance.

Forever impatient, angelic Mathias moved forward and stomped the ground with one giant feathered hoof. He snorted and tossed his thick black mane that hung well below his shoulders so that it landed on his broad back. His massive tail swished back and forth.

Seth eyed his equine companion and slid him a thought. *Simmer down, Mathias. All in good time.*

Kane released Seth's hand, disconnecting him from the white light that surrounded him. The two angels remained bathed in a heavenly aura. *To what do we owe this honor, my friend?*

Seth glanced at me and smiled. *We see Moon has healed from her wounds. We are glad no one was permanently injured.* His piercing eyes slid to Enzo. *You have done well to keep her safe, spirit wolf.*

Yes, Enzo had it well in hand. We just helped him with a few stray attackers. Kane crossed his arms and waited for an answer to his question.

Seth sighed. *I am afraid Enzo's prediction is correct. The worst is yet to come.*

Kane snorted and threw up his arms. *I can hardly wait to hear what more can be thrown at us.*

Seth glided closer to Kane and placed his arm around my master in comfort. The light hovered around my sire but didn't touch him. *The battle between good and evil is your and your kindred's destiny, Kane. You are God the Father's chosen warriors.*

Battle between good and evil? How can we represent God when we have been vilified throughout history as evil? Kane moved away from Seth's arm, and again the light slipped away from Kane when they disconnected.

Mathias snorted and responded without hesitation. *Lucifer wishes to overthrow God. That's why he tried to get control of you. He knows that the vampires are God's chosen warriors. Satan will throw all manner of evil and demons at you. It will be up to you and your kindred to save humanity from the fallen one's evil.*

Amidst the brothers' cries of anguish, Kane looked to Zandra, then me, and then back to Seth. *What do you mean we are God the Father's chosen warriors?*

Zandra bit her lip and emitted a throaty growl.

Zachary stepped forward. *That's absurd.*

Zeb joined his brother. *You must have lost your minds making your way here from heaven.*

Everyone groused about, shaking their heads. I looked to Enzo, and his sad eyes told me the angels spoke the truth.

This time, the first blood son, like God's only son, Jesus, will lead the battle against Lucifer.

Kane ran his fingers through his long hair as he often did when his mind was flooded with ideas.

Zandra walked to Kane's back and wrapped her arms around his waist. She leaned her head against him. I joined them. The others gathered around him.

"No." Kane stood firm, chin defiant, eyes burning. His spoken word rippled through the forest as an ultimatum.

Seth blinked.

Mathias stomped the ground, churning dirt. Mud chunks flew against the evergreen trees surrounding us. *You defy God?*

Why doesn't God just destroy Satan and not endanger innocent lives with all-out war? Zandra placed a delicate hand on Kane's chest.

I stepped in front of my master and his mate, willing to defend them should Mathias decide to attack. The Pegasus certainly seemed agitated enough to try.

Is this another one of God's tests on humanity's worthiness? Kane snorted. *If it is, it has become tiresome. I'm weary with fighting and putting my loved ones at risk.*

Seth's light glowed brightly. *God will reward you for fighting his battle for him, Kane. Just as Brogio had an ongoing wish, so do you. If you win the battle, He will grant it.*

Kane narrowed his eyes, and I pushed against his leg. *Everlasting peace is worth fighting for, Father.*

Peace? We can get long-lasting peace if we do this? Zandra searched her lover's eyes.

Do I have God's word on that, Seth? Kane raised his chin and stared at the heavenly messengers.

Mathias stomped his giant hoof, and the ground shook. *You dare to question God's word?*

Seth again rested his hand on Mathias' shoulder. *We're asking a lot, my impatient friend. His request is not unreasonable.* Turning to Kane, he nodded. *You have God's word.*

Kane looked around to each one of us.

The brothers nodded. Zylon declared, *It's time to kick some demon ass.*

Zandra smiled and nodded her head in agreement.

James stepped forward. *Your decision is my will, Kane.*

I pressed against my master. *Where you go, I follow.*

Enzo leaned against me. *I believe the word "ditto" is appropriate for me in this instance.*

Expect the unexpected, Seth warned as he and Mathias spread their enormous wings, faded, and disappeared.

I pressed close to my master. Enzo placed his head over my neck. Zandra pressed closer to Kane, and James and the brothers huddled close in an almost silent prayer.

Kane sighed. *Then, God give us strength.*

EPISODE TWO

LOVE FINDS A WAY

As we walked back from the forest, Zeb hastened his step and strode alongside Kane and Zandra.

Kane glanced at his hybrid vampire Lycan son and smiled. *You are curious about the angels, yes?*

Zeb nodded in the affirmative. *They are an overwhelming presence. We were all dumbstruck by the power that exuded from them.*

James and my brothers and I know that those two have helped us out on several occasions, but why did Seth, the angel, befriend a demon such as you in the first place? Is it because it was part of a greater plan?

Kane glanced at Zeb and put an arm around Zandra as they walked. *Perhaps in part. But Seth and I were friends long ago. Seth originally was an angel who fell from grace for the love of a human woman named Emma. Long story short, he became a white witch. Since I have dabbled in Wiccan ways, we became friends. After he fell, Emma died in an accident. But, actually, Hecate, goddess of witches, murdered the woman so that she could win Seth for herself.*

Zeb shook his head and kept pace with Kane's and Zandra's long strides. *What happened?*

At that time, every two hundred years, Hecate had the chance to woo and win a morally good man. Once they were mated, she could produce a demon seed and bring dark evil into the world. The witch disguised herself as a woman that could have been Emma's twin. She called herself Trivia and almost had him in her clutches. With the help of Brogio, Selene, Snow Blood, and his pack, we were able to trick her into revealing her true self to Seth.

So, how did he become an angel again? Zeb's rapt attention to Kane's every word told me that Seth's story enthralled him.

I glanced around to see the brothers all focused intently on Kane's information.

God created Seth with special love. He created an angel that embodied his own love of mankind. He made Seth to love humans equal to God's own love of them. Because Seth loved them so much, he became vulnerable to a human's love for him. He fixated on Emma and fell hopelessly in love with her. He gave up his immortality to be with her. When Seth fell from heaven so that he could be with Emma, God's heart was broken. He sent Mathias to be Seth's protector here on Earth. After his near-fatal encounter with Hecate and with some convincing from Mathias, God reinstated Seth because He wanted him back.

Zeb sighed. *I'm sure there's a lot more of that tale to tell.*

Yes. Kane hugged Zandra closer to him. *But right now, I have more important matters to attend.*

∞

Because of our connection, I sensed what matters consumed Kane's mind. Once we returned to the estate house, I followed Zandra and him into the large den, our primary meeting place in the house.

Enzo yawned and flopped down on his maroon velvet bed next to one of the twin maroon overstuffed chairs in front of the fireplace.

The brothers and James headed up the stairs to their respective bedrooms. I suspected they wanted to wash away the deeds of the night. I would save my grooming until after I had verified Kane's intent.

Zandra watched her siblings bounding up the stairs and laughed. *I feel the need of a bath, too.* She turned to her lover. *Want to join me?*

Kane hugged her. *In a minute. I have something to go over with Moon Blood.*

She smiled at him and looked down at me. *All right, but don't be long.*

We both watched as she skipped across the marbled black-and-white tile of the large entrance and headed up the circular stairs next to the front entry to the second floor.

Kane turned, went to the long wall-to-wall bar to the right of the perpetually burning oversized rock fireplace, and poured a glass of his vintage wine.

I looked around at the den with its wide mahogany plank floors covered with rich maroon and blue handmade Italian rugs. I loved to roll on the priceless artifacts, but James always chased me off.

Dark-stained cypress furniture filled this room. Beautiful artwork by the great masters lined the walls. Many of them were created by da Vinci, for whom Kane had apprenticed before he became a vampire.

I closed my eyes for a moment and reveled that this enormous nineteenth-century stone villa was my home. It housed fifteen bedrooms, containing art of all types from paintings and sculptures to expensive antique rugs. Even the brocade bedspreads were works of art. Each bedroom had its own ornate marble bathroom.

My mind wandered to our "sleeping room" with no windows and its king-sized four-poster bed, where Kane and

I slept safely during the daylight hours while Zandra, Enzo, and now Noble, who had replaced James as servant, took turns keeping watch. James, reluctant to give up his guardian role, persisted in joining them. The devil help anyone who tried to get through them to us.

Another flight of stairs from the second floor led to a rooftop balcony and a room with telescopes to watch the stars. Enzo and I often went up there to look over the red-tiled roof to view the surrounding hilly green panorama and vineyards of the Chianti Hills and the rows of ancient cypress trees that lined either side of the long drive through the fields to the house. Kane had built his estate hundreds of years ago just a short distance from Florence.

I remembered the first time Enzo had looked out over the extended forest where we met and told me we were fortunate to have the woods teeming with prey to feed upon. Kane and his progeny all followed Brogio's golden rule of never doing harm to humans or using them for sustenance on purpose.

While Kane fiddled with his assortment of wines at the bar, I padded into his large library and study, connected to a laboratory filled with experiments at different stages. The acrid smell of the lab always made me sneeze.

To squash my impatience at waiting for Kane to talk to me, I wandered into the recreation room with a wall-sized television, a complete entertainment center, pool table, and another bar. It opened through French doors to an elegant pool in the back of the house. A cabana outfitted with a table to seat twelve for serving meals sat poolside.

I was tempted to dive in, but Kane's voice slid through my mind and halted me. *Moon, come back to the den.*

He sat next to Enzo who pretended to sleep. Enzo never slept. He had no need to.

Yes, Master? You have something to tell me?

Come sit next to me, girl. He began rubbing my ears as I complied. I closed my eyes as he extended his fingernails into talons to give me a good scratch. His words caused me to abruptly open them.

We may all suffer the true death during this war, Moon. We have been lucky for too long.

I stood, shook my head and heavy white coat, and sat back down. *I understand.*

I decided on our walk back to commit to Zandra and make her my wife so that she will be assured of my love for her if one or both of us perish. I wanted you to be the first to know. You have always been and will forever be my special girl. I hope you will be happy for us.

Enzo sat up and stared at me over Kane's seat.

I snorted, *It's about time.*

∞

The estate house was ablaze with lights and merriment. Stringer lights zigzagged through the trees and overhead. Barrels of Kane's finest wines were served from numerous tables. Brogio had human blood flown in from Mexico and South America by the caseloads. Several long tables were loaded with steak, roast, chicken, pork, and lamb with assorted vegetables to sate the pallets of human and canine friends in attendance. I lapped at a bowl of my favorite O Neg that Zandra had set on the ground next to one of the tables.

The entire vampire nation, the majority in attendance as bats hanging in the trees all through the area between house and the winery, had come to witness the joining of Kane and Zandra. Brogio, the first vampire now human and Kane's sire, and his entire restored family gathered around the couple.

I finished my meal, pushing back the euphoria that always accompanied human nectar, and sauntered over to the group. Enzo dogged behind me. We were both curious to see how Zandra interacted with Brogio's wife. Even though Selene had always belonged to Brogio, Kane had loved her from the moment he'd met her. Zandra had often accused Kane of being attracted to her because she was the dark mirror image of Selene. Only his relationship with Zandra had helped my master overcome his unrequited love for his sire's wife.

As I approached, I noticed Zandra's golden eyes fixed on Selene's pale face. A smile spread across her olive-skinned face when Selene reached out and took both her hands. "I am so very happy that Kane has finally found a woman to match him in all ways! Congratulations, you two." The former vampire beamed at the couple.

Before I could hear Zandra's response, Joker, my uncle of sorts and pack member of my biological father, Snow Blood, knocked me down and rallied around me. My brothers and sister and the rest of Snow Blood's pack nudged me, nipped at me, and howled. Chase ran circles around me as Thor nipped at his back legs. Gaspar and Fergus stared at me watchfully. Their respective mates were busy gnawing at the bones Zandra's brothers kept feeding them as they gorged themselves at the meat table. Being hybrid vampire Lycans had not stopped their taste for meat by any means.

Zylon sent his concerns between bites to Zeb. *We have almost five hundred berserkers that we need to return to after this affair. Wish we didn't have to rush off.*

At the same time, Snow and Nova pushed through the swarm of yapping wolves and gave me a thorough licking from nose to tail. My only regret, now that their souls had all been restored, was not being able to communicate with them through telepathy. But it mattered not so much. From their greeting and the expressions of happiness on their faces, I knew how they felt.

I whirled around and called to Enzo. *Come. Meet my biological family.*

My spirit wolf sauntered over cautiously. After Enzo had been sniffed by everyone, we all lifted our heads toward the moon and howled. Enzo had been accepted on face value. No one had to explain to my family who he was. They knew.

Turning back to Kane and Zandra, I barked at the sight of the clan leaders that had joined them. Joseph, the mischievous one, slapped his hands, outstretched his arms to me, and fell to his knees. I rammed into his chest, knocking him over.

Leander, who was Brogio's second blood son, reached down and scratched my ears. *You are as elegant as always, Moon.*

Marco, Kane's cousin and progeny, was intent on conversation with Alexander. Both had been soldiers before being turned, and they always conferred on everything together.

Ian, as always, couldn't keep his eyes off his wife Leslie, who, with Marco's co-coven leader Mia, was quizzing Zandra.

For the sake of the humans in attendance, everyone broke protocol and spoke aloud.

Leslie gushed at Zandra. "Don't know how you did it. I thought Kane would never settle down."

Selene smiled at Zandra. "Tell us how Kane proposed."

The hybrid vampire Lycan almost glowed with the memory of it. "Well, it was just a week ago. We were in the bath together. I was leaning against his chest, and he asked."

"Details, Zandra, we women need details." Selene laughed as she spoke.

Zandra gave Kane a shy glance, unusual for her, and with his brief nod of the head, she went on. "He whispered in my ear that he loved me… and…"

"For God's sake, woman," Kane interrupted. "I told you that I loved you and that I wanted to make you the happiest hybrid in the world."

Zandra gave her fiancé a punch in the arm. "You did not. Let me tell it… Kane said that he had finally found the woman of his dreams and that he wanted us to be committed for eternity. Of course, I had been waiting to hear that ever since I met him."

Selene gave Zandra a big hug. "Congratulations on catching the most elusive bachelor in the world."

Never one to be shy, Leslie blurted out to Zandra for all to hear, "You really should let Mia and me be your bridesmaids."

"But I've just asked Selene to stand up with me." Zandra's golden orbs sparkled as she admired her newfound friend standing next to her.

Mia countered, "Why not let her be your maid of honor? Then we can be your bridesmaids."

Zandra swirled around. "Excellent suggestion. Let's go upstairs and get dressed."

The women left as Brogio and Kane rolled their eyes at each other.

"Let them have their fun." Kane laughed and turned to his sire. "I'm just happy that Zandra and Selene are going to get along."

Alexander turned to Brogio. "So, sire, I hear that you went online and got your license to officiate at the ceremony."

Marco cackled and slapped an apparently red-faced Brogio on the back.

Brogio drew his almost seven-foot frame up and glared down at Marco. It became immediately apparent that even though he no longer headed the vampire nation, Brogio would not tolerate disrespect from his former underlings.

Marco bowed his head and stretched out his hand to the original vampire. "I meant no disrespect. I am sorry. I think it's wonderful that you would marry your first blood son."

"But who else," Kane interjected, "but the father of our race."

Brogio's violet eyes scanned Marco's bowed head. He pushed back a long strand of silver-white hair, and then took the vampire's hand. "See that you never disrespect me, Marco." He looked up at Alexander as well. "I might no longer have vampire strength, but over the millennia that I have lived, I still retain some pretty impressive skills. I'm not afraid to use them."

"Yes," Kane interjected, "Father is still the most impressive swordsman I've ever met."

James glided over and bowed to his former master.

"Thank you, Kane." Brogio placed a hand on his former servant's shoulder. "Except, James can give me a run for my money. Trained him myself."

James smiled and touched the broad sword he now always carried.

Turning to Brogio, Kane put a hand on the man's shoulder. "Now, what say we go into my study for a while, and you can tell me how I can survive this marriage?"

I looked over at Enzo, and we joined my hybrid-wolf family while they gnawed on bones. Zandra's brothers hovered over the beef table gnawing on pieces of meat and continued throwing the bones to my hybrid brothers and sister. Soon, Zandra returned and tapped me on the shoulder. *Come, my wolf sister. You didn't think you wouldn't be one of my bridesmaids as well? We need to have you try on the flower collar Selene has made for you.*

∞

The full floral bouquet of yellow and blue flowers that circled my neck and tickled my face made me sneeze. I stood next to Selene in the den in front of the fireplace with Leslie and Mia to my other side. The women were dressed in long silver gowns with blue and yellow ribbons and flowers in their hair. I noted even their shoes were silver in color and sneezed again.

For this one occasion, Kane had the servants put out the flames in the fireplace, clean it, and fill it with flowers and greenery. The room's furniture had been removed and set with gold chivari cushioned chairs on either side of an aisle with a gold lamé runner.

Kane stood across from Selene and wore the gold brocade tuxedo jacket that she and Brogio had gifted to him some years ago. He had changed the black pants for gold lamé pair. His long dark hair was pulled back in a knot at the base of his neck and tied with a gold ribbon.

He had chosen Snow Blood as his best man. The white husky had history with my sire, and Kane wanted to honor him by asking him to stand up with him. While Snow was no longer a vampire, he retained an intuitive communication with his family, which included Kane. All Kane had to do was ask, and Snow was happy to stand with the creature he called his vampire brother. He wore his usual red collar but had been fitted with a gold lamé vest that covered his chest and back.

As the celebrant to officiate the wedding, Brogio wore a long black robe with a gold lamé stole that hung from around his neck. His long silvery white hair hung loose around his broad shoulders. He held the Vampire Bible in his hand.

Zandra came down the circular stairs where Zeb, dressed in all-black leather, awaited to escort her to her groom. The other brothers wearing identical black leather followed and took their chairs in the front row.

I had to admit that Zandra's hulking brothers were quite a study in human masculinity. All of them looked as if they could star in the superhero movies they loved to watch on Kane's large television.

The coven leaders, James in a spotless white tuxedo, wolves, and hybrids were interspersed throughout the room.

Everyone gasped when Zandra first appeared. The gold of her dress matched her eyes. It sparkled with sewn-in blue rhinestones. She wore a garland of yellow and blue flowers atop her long flowing black hair that reached down to her waist. Her gold shoes sparkled as she walked.

I wondered how she had pulled all this together in a week, but I'm a hybrid wolf. What do I know about creating weddings?

Thinking briefly about wedding arrangements, I soon was distracted by Enzo's unblinking eyes and frozen body as he lay facing me to the side of the chairs on the left. When his eyes refocused, he looked at me and warned, *Satan has just released the brothers' hold on the berserkers they have kept at bay. More have joined them. Maybe a thousand. The flesh eaters are coming for us now.*

∞

Enzo made his warning heard to all. Kane instantly began to remove his jacket and pants and shouted, "We are under attack!"

Zandra followed suit and stripped off her wedding gown. Pandemonium swirled throughout the room as every vampire and shapeshifter rushed to remove clothing and prepared to transform.

We found no time to protect or hide our human family.

A swarm of the legendary Viking fighters crashed through the front door of the estate. The front windows on either side of the door exploded with werewolf berserkers who had harnessed the power of their chosen fighting animals and wore bear, wolf, or hog skins. Their deformed troll-like faces were swollen with rage. They could tear down every living thing in their path until the end of battle and had the capability to rip their enemies apart with their bare hands.

I had to get to as many of them as I could and felt my body morph into my inner demon as I crashed into the stinking bodies of our attackers. I made a swath through the enemy swarm biting and dropping them like flies. Enzo ran by my side leaning against me, protecting the one side of me. We pushed our way to the outside. I kept biting flesh as we went. An arm, an ankle, a tendon, everything was fair game. I left them to die in my wake. My spirit wolf unhinged his jaw, baring serrated teeth. The effect was disturbing. He tilted his head, raking a berserker along his side. A wet splat pronounced his guts spilling on the ground. Enzo raised his head and slit the throat of another wolfman. When I glimpsed the berserker, his head rolled off his neck and bounced on his chest.

Behind me, I heard bones cracking. Turning, I witnessed Kane sprout wings and red scales. His neck grew long, and horns sprouted from his face. His body grew to an enormous size, and his red eyes flashed and sent out a glaring warning to all who would approach him. He moved forward forcing out the balance of those who were trying to swarm the house.

As he began to rise into the air, a filthy flesh eater grabbed a diamond scale with his teeth and squeezed, but his jaw wouldn't close around the dragon skin. The flesh eater pulled at the scale, but it wouldn't come loose.

I felt dismay at my master being attacked but shouldn't have worried. Now outside, he roared past me and flooded hundreds of enemies with fire. One by one, as soon as the fire hit, their death howls pierced the night air drowning our enemies with dread. Many tried to turn and run only to be devoured by dragon fire.

A giant standing more than ten feet appeared from behind enemy lines. It had to be the ugliest creature I had ever witnessed. Covered in stinking, matted hair, its jaw hung to its chest revealing razor-sharp teeth. Its body hunched and then stretched, swinging at the Kane dragon.

One swipe grabbed a scaly leg and yanked, crashing Kane to the ground.

My heart went into my throat, and I sprang forward to assist. Before I could reach him, the dragon had leaped up and covered the monstrosity with liquid flames as he soared up to the sky again.

The giant swirled, waving his arms in agony. His cries drowned out the battle roar until he fell face-first and took out some fifty of his own comrades.

We circled, biting our way to Zandra, now an unrecognizable demon with protruding fangs, shaggy black hair, claws, and snakelike yellow eyes. She sprang on a group of ferocious attackers and sliced their jugulars in two quick swipes. Her thoughts sang through my mind. *That's what you get for ruining my wedding day, you bastards!*

Another managed to claw her arm.

How dare you. This is her wedding day. I jumped on him and bit into his chest, ripping out his heart. *I take your heart for breaking hers.*

James, his white tuxedo spotless, grew taller as he calmly slashed his way through ten flesh eaters. It was unnerving to watch him slowly approach each intended victim as he blocked surrounding attacks with just his sword. Upon reaching his prey, he efficiently left them headless. Many of his enemies took a step back from him in fear of his calculated demeanor only to fall under his sword.

Enzo and I moved to the other side of James and saw Brogio block a surprise attack on me from behind. Wielding a broad sword that had been hanging on the wall, he cut my would-be attacker almost in half. Selene came behind him cutting down another who attempted to leap onto Brogio's back with the broad sword from the opposite wall.

Fighting back-to-back and circling and slashing, Brogio and Selene managed to cut down about twenty attackers before each sustained minor injury.

Snow Blood and his entire pack went for the jugulars of individual werewolves, attacking them from behind as more swarmed to try and overcome Brogio and Selene as they fought their way out into a more open space.

The coven leaders took to the skies as black dragons and joined Kane's red dragon, raining fire down on the enemies. In another section of the estate, thousands of vampire bats swarmed the enemy on the ground. I took pause at the sight of groups of some five hundred creatures of the night ganging up on individual flesh eaters and biting, tearing, and ripping off the skin of these frightening warriors, whose screams pierced through the night air. Once prone and sucked dry in seconds, they were left for another victim.

Enzo and I rushed, avoiding the fire that now covered the forest and the vineyards, and ferreted out attackers lurking in the woods. Snow Blood, Nova, and the wolves joined us, and as wolves work, they targeted one individual at a time and ambushed each as a pack. Little was left of these individuals once the pack was upon them.

Broken body parts, ripped-out hearts, decapitated heads, and half-burned berserkers, along with piles of the ash of incinerated creatures, littered the front of the estate.

Landing momentarily, Kane and his coven leaders morphed into what could only be described as monster-sized lizards. They shed their black and red scales for bright green. Each had a dramatic crest with spines on their heads, backs, and tails. Their crest pointed upward to form rounded shapes. I wondered why, and Kane shot the answer to me telepathically. *Water dragons.*

They took to the skies, dumping water on the vineyards and surrounding trees to protect the estate. The damage was substantial, but he had rebuilt before. As they circled through the fields and trees, Brogio, Selene, James, the brothers, the wolf pack, the bats, Enzo, and I ended stray attackers.

Snow Blood and his wolves gathered around Enzo and me as we watched the dying fire. Enzo turned to me. *I estimate we just destroyed a thousand flesh-eating werewolves.*

Yes, and did you see how well Brogio and his family fought?

Enzo snorted. *Yes. And James impressed me as well.*

I licked his face. *You always impress me.*

Then, my thoughts turned sad as I thought of this unhappy ending to what had been planned as a joyous occasion.

∞

My biological sire, his wolf family, Enzo, and I soon rejoined everyone in the den.

Kane immediately set out healing the injuries that Brogio and Selene had sustained. To safeguard them against taking in vampire-contaminated blood, he used his healing tongue to close the wounds. It was one of his many gifts, and one that Enzo appeared to possess as well. He had expressed to me and my siblings long ago that his lick could heal most external wounds.

Noble had already gathered the multiple silent servants dressed in black to clear the dead debris from the den at the estate. This was a task to which they had become accustomed both inside and outside the house. I knew from experience that at some time during the day as we rested, they would burn the remains and clean the room. Blood covered the floor and the walls. Even the ceiling had been splattered with the enemies' black blood. I had learned from watching them before that they protected themselves from being contaminated by the black blood of shifters and vampires. They reminded me of people wearing biohazard suits, headgear, and gloves that I had seen once with Zandra's brothers in a television movie. Yes, I liked to watch television and did when we had time with the hybrid vampire Lycan brothers.

After attending to the humans, Kane finished checking Zandra for injury. Her arm, deeply clawed, had already begun to heal on its own; a benefit of being a hybrid. My sire then came and gave a thorough inspection to Snow Blood, Nova, their pack, and me.

They are all well, Kane. Enzo sat back on his haunches. *I made sure no harm came to our girl, Snow, Nova, and the wolf pack.*

Brogio wiped at his torn clothing now spoiled with blood. He joined us with Selene on his heels. Her silver dress was ruined and in tatters. "Thank God we didn't bring our son with us," she whispered to her husband.

I thought of little Adam and felt gratitude that he was safe at home in Nova Scotia with his nanny and a horde of vampires that Leander had sent to guard him in his parents' absence.

Kane, do you know the origin of this attack? Brogio's violet eyes searched the dark orbs of his first blood son, who, like all vampires, could read the thoughts of humans.

Yes, Father. He looked around the den. *First, I apologize to everyone, and I have a story to tell you about why we were attacked.*

I watched Brogio's and Selene's expressions as they listened to Kane's retelling of what the angels had told us. Their faces shifted from anger to sadness.

Alexander and Marco jammed their fists into the palms of their hands almost simultaneously. The other coven leaders milled about in agitation, speaking aloud. Their angry voices escalated. "Why does it always fall on us?"

"Can there be enough of us to fight off Satan's evil?"

Leander's calm voice broke through. "It is simple. We will fight. I for one am tired of these endless attacks. Let's end it once and for all."

Brogio stepped forward and placed a large hand on Kane's shoulder. "Selene, Snow Blood, and his pack, and I will stay to fight with you."

Kane pulled away from him. "No! No! You are in mortal danger now. You no longer have vampire defenses. I won't be at my best if I have to worry about you being harmed or worse."

Brogio threw back his head and ran his hands through his silver-white hair now stained with black blood. "You have no say in the matter. Didn't you notice we held our own here?"

Zandra walked to Kane and slid her hand in one of his. "Like you won't worry about everyone here, human, vampire, or canine? You will worry no matter who is fighting."

Kane shrugged and mumbled, "Guess you're right."

Selene moved in between her husband and Kane and looped an arm through each of theirs. "Now. What are we going to do about this wedding?"

Kane eyed his intended bride. "Why, we finish the deed."

"Now?" Selene looked around the ruined room and the tattered guests. Having ripped their clothing when they transformed, the coven leaders stood naked. The brothers' leather suits hung in shreds on them, while James' perfectly clean white suit stood out. Nothing was left of my floral collar or Snow Blood's vest. Man and beast were covered in battle debris.

Zandra put her hands on her hips. "Yes, *now*. I may never get another chance to marry this big lug! We might both suffer the true death tomorrow." She twirled around, picked up her wedding dress, and stepped into it.

While Kane retrieved his brocade jacket and gold pants and Brogio refitted his robe and scarf-like stole, the servants passed around warm towels for wiping off/removing the blood of the battle to everyone else.

James cleaned up Snow and me as best he could and then tended to the rest of the wedding party.

The naked coven leader bridesmaids stood proudly next to Selene and her splattered dress.

Brogio cleared his deep throat. "I speak for the Storm Goddess. Tonight, we are gathered under the cloak of Mother Night and the eye of Sister Moon to bond these two, Kane de Medici and Zandra Moretti, in eternal companionship. From this night forth, they shall walk together in eternity, their cold hands clasped, their still hearts possessed completely by the other. This is not a vow entered lightly by those who shall not be touched by the withering fingers of time. The bond is unbreakable. Their blood is already one. Should one be struck down, so shall fall the other, but also so bonded, their strengths shall be joined and the love in their un-beating hearts shall fill dead flesh with impossible warmth."

Brogio paused and instructed, "Turn to face each other so that you may look upon the visage that shall be one with you for the rest of time. Kane, speak 'I will' after my speech is ended.

"Kane, will you, first blood son of Brogio, swear by the very un-life that fills you, by the stolen blood that pounds through you veins, to give yourself completely, utterly, without question or doubt to this mate? To hunt with, offering always the choicest prey first to her before taking it yourself because you love her?"

I watched my sire as he looked into the hybrid vampire Lycan's eyes. They were brimming with blood tears and love.

He answered, "Always. I will."

Brogio turned to the bride.

"Zandra, speak 'I will' after my speech is ended as Kane did."

Brogio paused, looked at them both, and then proceeded. "Zandra, will you, daughter of King Lycaon, firstborn progeny of the original werewolf and hybrid vampire Lycan born of Kane, swear by the very un-life that fills you, by the stolen blood that pounds through your veins, to give completely, utterly, without question or doubt to this mate? To hunt with, forsaking the choicest prey even when offered because you love him? To spend your days of slumber protected in his arms? If he hungers, to feed him from your own veins until he is quenched? To use your body to shade him should the hateful sun seek to touch him? And, if he is taken from you, will you remain by his ashes as yours mingle with his own?"

Zandra's tears spilled down her face like streaks of tar. She nodded and then answered, "I will."

Brogio nodded. "May the shadows hold you both safe in its velvet folds as you begin this journey together that shall not end until time itself has no meaning. The rings now. Please exchange the rings."

Kane pulled out from his jacket pocket a beautiful band encrusted with bloodred rubies and diamonds and placed it on his bride's finger.

Brogio then continued, "Do you, Kane, take Zandra to be your Queen?"

Kane answered, "I do."

Zandra turned to Selene who handed her a platinum band covered in bloodred rubies that she pulled from her tattered pocket. Zandra placed it on Kane's finger.

Brogio turned to her. "Do you, Zandra, take Kane to be your King?"

Zandra's voice sounded loud and clear. "I do!"

Brogio brought out a bloodred sash and tied their hands together.

"Kane, you may now bite your bride."

My sire nudged Zandra's dark hair from her neck and bit into it.

"Zandra, you may now bite your groom."

My sire's mate did the same.

Brogio pronounced, "It is done. What the darkness, evil, and night has brought together, let no mortal, demon, nor spirit tear apart. You are now joined together. You may kiss."

At this point, I buried my eyes in Selene's dress. I heard Zylon shout, "Get a room!"

And then laughter and applause ensued.

Partying commenced until the sun began to creep over the hills and the vampire bats and coven leaders went to the special catacombs Kane had built centuries ago for them. Brogio and his pack went to their guest rooms, and the day-walking hybrid brothers positioned themselves throughout the grounds to keep watch. James, Noble, and Enzo positioned themselves outside our sleeping room where Zandra would join us for the daylight hours.

Just as I padded over to the bedroom door, Enzo shook his head and shot me a warning. *Human infighting has begun in Florence.*

EPISODE THREE

THE UNDEAD ATTEMPT TO RULE

As night fell, I awoke to their lovemaking. Jumping off the bed and slinking out the door, I wanted to give Kane and his bride a few moments of joy before they had to deal with the next onslaught. I nudged open the door and met Enzo's golden eyes staring at me.

This having to sleep during the daylight is quite inconvenient. He sat back and licked his chops with his pink tongue. *James took initiative and went into Florence to verify my vision. Everyone is gathered downstairs to hear his report as soon as he returns.*

Before I could reply or get into the hallway, Kane's words filled my head. *Go ahead to the den. We will join you shortly.*

Noble stood up from his chair beside the bedroom door and gave me a slight bow. "Good morning, Moon. I have had my assistants prepare breakfast for everyone."

I noticed he had done away with the man bun as Kane had requested. The tall, lean young man now wore his blond hair down around his shoulders. He dressed in the customary black clothing of all Kane's servants. His only distinction was a white bowtie he had placed around the collar of his shirt. Perhaps a sign of head servant?

I concentrated and tried speaking to him telepathically as I had learned to do with James. *Is everyone in the dining room?*

A smile spread across his face, and he answered, "Yes!"

My chest swelled at my accomplishment, and I sauntered down the stairs with Enzo behind me. *Perhaps if I have made James and Noble hear me, then I can communicate with Brogio, Selene, and Snow Blood's brood?*

Enzo shoved me with his nose. *Yes, you can. You've always had that ability. Just do it now.*

Padding into the den, I noticed that all the coven leaders lounged with large glasses of human blood.

Joseph raised his glass to me and smiled, and I went over and nudged his hand for an ear scratch.

Turning toward the dining room, I noticed that Zandra's brothers, along with Brogio and Selene, were enjoying a hearty breakfast. If I had been human, I would have laughed at the sight of the Z brothers going at it in a two-fisted manner with large legs of beef in one hand and large mugs of human blood in the other. It had to be the best of both worlds for them.

Wanting to try out my newly found ability, I marched over to Brogio, closed my eyes, and thought, *Kane and Zandra will be down shortly.*

Brogio threw back his head and laughed. "I would hope they would take some private time before joining us, Moon."

You heard me?

"We all heard you, dear girl." Selene stood up from her chair and knelt next to me. "You are quite an accomplished and superior being."

Snow Blood and his pack, who were scattered around the den and dining room, began to bark and howl.

They can hear me, too?

My biological sire got up from the other side of his master's chair and gave me a thorough licking.

"He is quite proud of you, Moon." Brogio grinned and gave my butt a good scratching.

James burst through the door just as Kane and Zandra reached the bottom of the stairs. "It's true! It's happening now, all over Florence! All over Italy!"

Come in. Kane took James by the shoulder and escorted him into the den where we all joined. *Now that Moon has established she can communicate with all telepathically, and since I've just been waiting for her to realize it, let's now resume doing so. We don't want to give away our secrets to Satan's prying ears. All of us, of course, can read Brogio, Selene, Snow Blood, and his pack's thoughts with their permission.*

The two humans nodded their agreement, and Snow Blood barked his acceptance.

Kane turned to James, handed his former servant-turned-vampire a large glass of blood from the bar, and sighed. *Tell us.*

James gulped down his repast, rolled back his deep-gray eyes in momentary ecstasy, and then began to pace. *It's a nightmare. An aggressive breed of humans… no… more like zombies… are slaughtering the uninfected townspeople. As soon as they are bitten, if they aren't eaten completely, they too become undead creatures intent on consuming everything in their path.*

Zandra stepped forward and placed her hand on James' arm. *How widespread is it?*

The whole city. I called an old vendor of mine in Venice. He has managed to hide himself and his family away from harm so far. He said it has spread throughout all of Italy, according to his sources.

Kane stood in front of the now lit fireplace and stroked his chin.

We all stared expectantly at him.

After the silence finally got to me, I closed my eyes and sent a message so all could understand. *Father, if this has spread throughout Italy...*

Brogio's thoughts merged with mine...*then it would take a major miracle for us to be able to overcome that many rabid beings.*

Kane raised his hand. *I think I have a solution. Rather than fight physically, let's combat this intellectually.*

Zandra smiled and took two long strides to his side. *I knew you'd have a solution.* She pinched his arm. *But what in the world is it?*

I need to create a way to neutralize the infection, to render it ineffective. Something that cures or kills the infected but doesn't harm the noninfected. He began to pace back and forth until Brogio laughed aloud.

What?

You have become more and more like me in your mannerisms. It just struck me. Brogio turned to Snow Blood and grinned, and my biological sire barked in agreement.

But... Kane turned and focused his dark eyes on Enzo and me, *it will require someone to take great risk.*

What do you need, Father? I padded over and rubbed my body against Kane's knee.

I need someone to secure a blood sample from one of those infected beings. It's a dangerous task. He rubbed my head.

I will go, I immediately offered.

She won't go without me. Enzo walked to my side.

They can't do this alone! Zandra interjected. *I will go with them.*

Kane turned to her, took her hand, folded it under his arm, and patted it. *No. I will go with them. They will need a way to carry the blood back here. They'll need a pair of hands.*

Everyone instantly began to argue.

I interjected, *I can morph into a human as soon as I take down one of the infected creatures.*

Alexander appealed for the coven leaders. *We can't risk you being harmed, Kane. It would end us all.*

Let me go, James offered. *I am the most dispensable.*

No. Each of the brothers crowded around Kane and Zandra.

Zachary spoke first. *We should go.*

We can morph into dogs and then convey the blood in a container in human form, Zander added.

No need for Moon and Enzo to go. Zoltan's kind golden eyes rested on my face.

You forget. Kane sighed. *I can do that, as well as Moon Blood. She can become anything. And I'm willing to bet with the venom in her blood, she might just be immune to the infectious bite of these zombies.*

Brogio stepped forward, and Kane stopped him with the palm of his hand shoved against his sire's chest. *Don't even suggest it. You and Selene are the most vulnerable.*

Brogio threw up his hands in exasperation and stomped off to the bar to pour a glass of wine.

Leander, Marco, and the rest of the coven leaders stepped forward. Before they could speak, Kane glared at them and shut them down.

Zandra put her arm around her husband. *Face it. Any vampire in this room can shapeshift into anything we want. I don't think you or Moon Blood should be put at risk. You are the mastermind, and Moon's deadly bite has saved us many a time. Let me and a few of my brothers go.*

Kane ran his hands through his hair. *Everyone wait here. I need to do some research on the potion I need to make. I suspect I know why Moon needs to go, but I want to double-check.*

∞

An hour later, Kane gathered us all back in the den.

It's as I suspected, and it's complicated. What we need is a sample of the infected blood mingled at the moment of contact with the venom in Moon's bite. Her venom will cancel out the infected blood and cause her no harm. If she can bite off a chunk of one of the zombies, and we can get it back here, I can make the potion from that.

I smiled inwardly. The white witch in him was masterminding this potion.

He turned to James. *Are these zombies rotting corpses, or do they just look like humans with rabies?*

They aren't rotting corpses. That's what is so insidious about it. You can't tell they are infected until they try to bite you. James raked a hand though his now-white hair.

Then, I should be able to make both a cure and a preventive rolled into one. He turned to me. *Still want to do this?*

I barked and headed for the door with Enzo behind me.

Kane's mental message halted me. *Not so fast, girl. We'll take one of the cars to Florence.*

This time, Brogio wouldn't be silenced. *Kane, if you go, and something happens to you, you risk everyone in this room dying except my family. Do you want to take that risk?*

James silently approached my sire. *Please, sir.* He turned quickly to Zandra. *Please, my sire. Let me do this. Let me prove my worth. You have granted me a life as a vampire hybrid Lycan. I can shift and be whatever is needed, and together, Enzo and I can protect Moon. Let me go.*

Kane recognized in James the need to prove his worth. He had felt the same with his own sire, Brogio.

Zandra nodded to Kane.

He sighed. *All right, James. But if anything happens to her, or you, I'll end you.* He smiled at his weak attempt at a joke. *Take the town car.*

∞

I enjoyed the silence as James drove us to Florence. Enzo sat up front next to him, and I watched the cypress tree-lined road. City lights bathed the sky with a moonlike glow. As we drew closer to the city, I cringed at the site of a few dead humans lying slaughtered like roadkill by the wayside. Throats ripped, holes in their chests where a heart should be, half-eaten brains, gray matter oozing from ears, they would not reanimate. Further down the road, I observed seemingly intact men and women struggling to rise from the ground.

Enzo turned back to me. *The ones who rise have but a single bite on their neck.*

Yes, I snorted. *It's like a vampire's kiss. Satan mocks us by creating these creatures to use the "embrace" to turn him an army.*

The "embrace"? James interjected.

Kane taught me that a vampire can only "turn" a person by purposely using the embrace, as Zandra did with you. Like Kane did with me. I stood up in the back and hung my head over the front seat. *These creatures are biting and then feeding their own blood to their victims. The roadkill we saw further back were just used for food, like we decimate our prey.*

James turned around and gave me a look. *How do you know all this?*

I licked my chops. *Because I am irrevocably connected to Kane like no other. He has linked his mind to mine and shared much of his knowledge with me. He has wished this to be so, and it is.*

James turned back and remained silent.

As we drove on and into the city, we observed a man, obviously a friend, lover, or husband, wave to a woman. She ran to him, feeling safe. Perhaps having been in hiding and waiting for him. He embraced her and then bit into her neck. I saw her mouth open in a scream as her legs gave way underneath her.

I imagined she would soon rise and help him do the same to other family members, and I shuddered at the thought of how quickly this infection could destroy humanity.

James drove into the Limited Travel Zone and historical part of Florence near the Hall of Five Hundred. Kane had explained to me that because Florence is heavily pedestrian, a special permit is required to drive through it. On this night, no law enforcement stood to check for cars. James pulled over and stopped.

What's your plan, Moon? James turned to me.

I will find an infected one and secure the sample. Both of you wait here for me. Please open the door. I twirled and faced the back door in expectation.

No, Enzo objected and leaned over the seat. *I go with you. James stays here.*

As you wish, Enzo. I hopped back and forth on my front feet anxious to get started.

We will all go. James jumped out of the car and opened the front door. He leaned in to look at me. *I have my sword for protection. I want to avoid being infected by being bitten by them, and Kane will be true to his word and end me if you don't come back unharmed.*

I snorted as the hybrid opened my door for me. I took off on a dead run, with Enzo and James, sword drawn, on my back end.

I scooted through the Palazzo Vecchio, which houses the Hall of Five Hundred. The ground floor contained astonishing courtyards, decorated with frescoes and fountains. The entire place was a labyrinth of chambers, apartments, terraces, and courtyards. I expected one or more of the undead to leap out from behind a fountain any moment.

I heard guttural growls and paused behind a tall statue. Enzo and James hovered behind me.

Five human figures walked with purpose from a nearby apartment. Nothing in their appearance indicated they were anything but normal men.

I had to be sure these were my targets, so I leapt from behind the statue and slowly approached.

They turned in unison and locked onto me.

One veered away from the group and moved with purpose toward me.

I stopped, sat back on my haunches, and waited.

His eyes gleamed at me, and I felt a ripple of danger run through my spine. He reached for me, and I sprang, knocking him down and landing on his chest. I growled and bit deep into his chest, releasing my venom and ripping a large chunk of him away.

He tried to snap at me, baring sharp fangs, but began to convulse and foam before he stopped moving.

The other four converged on me, but James ran forward and lopped two of their heads off before they could touch me. Enzo, spirit animal as he was, appeared immune to the infection of the other two and ripped out hearts with his razor-like teeth, first from the one, and then the other.

James turned to me, holding out the container Kane had given us to secure the sample, and I spit the chunk into it. Just as I did, the creature I had taken down reanimated.

The man stood, staggered for a moment, and shook his head, holding his torn chest.

Before I could blink, several infected creatures emerged and attacked the man and took him down. His screams rang through the air as they ripped at him.

GO! James' thought screamed at me. *We have what we need!*

We ran with more infected creatures on our trail. With vampire speed, we dodged others who sprang out from hidden doorways or statues. Some just stood in our way and tried to grab us as we dashed by them. One infected tried to grab James' foot only to find himself without a hand as

James slashed at each attacker with his sword. He lopped off heads, hands, and arms as we flew by.

Enzo amazed me as he jumped over our attackers and tore out throats and spat them out as he went.

I increased my speed, becoming a blur that none could see.

We outran them, reached the car, and leapt in before some fifty of them crashed into the town car, which was outfitted like an armored vehicle with protective shields for the windows and body.

Most of them hit the automobile so hard that it knocked them back away from us.

James roared out of the Palazzo Vecchio with more than ten of them hanging on to the doors, back fenders, and hood. He swerved throwing the three on the doors off into nearby buildings. When he slammed on the brakes, he sent three more flying off the hood. Then, he plowed over them. The remaining ones lost their grip as we bumped over the bodies of their fallen comrades.

We sped off toward the Chianti Hills.

I leaned over the seat, being careful not to step on James' sword that he'd thrown on the floor in the back. *Am I seeing things, or did the creature I take out come alive again as a normal human?*

I saw it. James accelerated the car.

It appears—Enzo licked my face—*that your venom and his blood infection mingled and cured him. That must be why he was attacked by the other creatures.*

I sat back. *I hope you are right, Enzo.*

∞

Kane inspected me thoroughly for bodily harm, took the bloody pulp in the airtight container that James handed him, and retreated to his laboratory with a simple, *Well done.*

The rest of our family surrounded us wanting to make sure the three of us were all right and then begged for all the details.

After we had gone over what had transpired a few times, Zandra offered everyone a glass of wine. As she set down a bowl of my favorite O Neg, she began to formulate a plan. *While Kane is working on his potion, we need to come up with a distribution plan.*

Kane, as always reading everyone's minds, stuck his head into the den. *Think distribution through drinking water.* Then, he turned and disappeared back to his work.

Brogio sipped his wine and began to pace. *If this thing has spread throughout the country, we need to tap into the nation's main water supply. Most Italian cities get their drinking water from rivers. For instance, Florence gets most of its drinking water from the Arno.*

And Naples, my territory, Joseph offered with excitement, *receives its drinking water through the Western Campania Aqueduct from the Gari River.*

Rome gets its water from the aqueducts. Alexander knew his region well.

Yes. Brogio ran his fingers through his silver-white hair, and his violet eyes flashed. *So, between the coven leaders, Zandra, and her brothers, we divide up the country and get this potion infiltrated into the water supply. Kane said what he would create would affect the undead but not the uninfected. If we can stop it in Italy, perhaps we can protect the rest of the world. With the wine distribution that Kane and I have, we can put it in our product shipped internationally as a preventive.*

I padded forward next to Brogio. *But what if these creatures don't drink water?*

Kane's sire patted me on the head. *You are such a smart girl. Perhaps your father has already thought of that. Let's wait and see.*

Before the sun rose, Kane joined us. *I have it. Now I just need to mass produce it for all of you to distribute.* He smiled at me. *I analyzed what components in our blood attract them. It's in the formula to draw them to drink the water*—he glanced at Brogio—*and humans will be drawn to drink the wine. None of them will be able to resist it.*

One other subject nagged at me. *Why won't my venom kill the humans?*

Kane smiled. *Because my formula neutralizes it.*

Everyone laughed. The brothers slapped each other on the back, and Snow Blood sauntered over to Kane and looked up at him. His thoughts made me pant and smile. *You used a bit of magic, didn't you, my brother?*

He scratched the husky's head. *Just some white magic, with maybe a dark spell or two, in the name of God the Father.*

∞

As the sun dipped behind the horizon, Brogio met Kane, Zandra, and me at our sleeping-room door. *Kane, I contacted a large pharma laboratory that I funded years ago. The CEO owes me a favor, and he's frightened out of his mind about what's happening anyway. He knows what's at stake. His COO went home early the other day and was infected on the way. He spread the disease to his wife, but his oldest daughter witnessed it and managed to escape and gather her family and get them to the pharma headquarters. The CEO was almost infected himself when a zombie attacked the worker letting in the COO's family. He pulled the family to safety but was unable to reach his worker who was devoured before his eyes on the other side of the glass sliding doors. Horrified, he ordered the lead security doors lowered to prevent any break-ins. He is more than willing to mass produce the formula, no questions asked. We need to get it to him right away.*

Kane took his sire by the arm, and they descended the stairs with the rest of us in pursuit. *Is it the one in Rome?*

Alexander met us at the bottom of the stairs. *Yes. I know the CEO. Brogio introduced us years ago. I'll take it and have it there before eleven tonight.*

I've made the arrangements for Alexander to do the drop-off, Brogio interjected.

It won't be safe for him to go on foot, Kane warned. *Who knows what one of these creatures can do to us?*

That's why—Brogio grinned exposing perfect white teeth—*one of your company helicopters is picking him up in the next ten minutes. The pharma company has a helipad on the roof of their building. They'll make the transfer there.*

Damn, it's great to be surrounded by a team of problem-solvers. Kane smiled around the room then turned to his blood father. *How long before he has it ready?*

Twenty-four hours max. Alexander gave an enthusiastic thumbs-up. *He's waiting in the building to meet me as soon as I arrive.*

Once they turned on the news and saw what was happening, Brogio added, *they barricaded the building and didn't let anyone in or out to prevent infection within. He nearly had an employee riot on his hands until they realized they couldn't protect their families.*

Selene handed Kane and Zandra glasses of blood and placed a bowl for me on the floor. It was AB, not my favorite, but still good. She stood and motioned to everyone around the room. *Brogio has arranged for Alexander to pick up the potion by helicopter as soon as it is ready. It will be stored in individually contained packages for everyone here to distribute to the waters.*

Brogio poured a glass of wine. *I've already arranged to have it bottled in my wines. You'll just need to do the same, Kane.*

I lapped up my blood nectar and listened to the conversation. As I finished, I noticed Enzo's frozen body.

The whirl of helicopter blades twirled above the estate. Alexander's ride had arrived.

I marched to Enzo as his eyes refocused. *What?*

My spirit wolf shook his body. *They are here. I wondered how long it would be.*

Infected ones are here? Kane looked at Enzo and then took Alexander by the arm and pressed the sealed vial into his hand.

They rushed through the door and ran for the copter as it landed between the house and the winery. Twenty feet from the door, they were surrounded by some twenty infected.

James and I were first to react and ran into the fray. I bit into one after the other, bringing them down with my venom, and James wielded his sword. He danced off the back of one, ran his blade through the stomach of another, twisted the hilt, and cut the zombie in half. In a flash he finished it off by swinging up, slicing off its head. As more attackers rushed from the trees, the rest of the group stood in awe as the four of us—Kane, Alexander, James, and I—whirled around them, slicing, dicing, and chewing. As soon as the ones I had bitten tried to rise as reanimated humans, their former counterparts would attack them. I bit, Kane and Alexander ripped off heads, and James sliced them up.

Enzo joined the fight as more zombies rushed us, teeth snapping and eyes glazed with deadly intent. One jerked toward me just missing my snout. I sidestepped and bit off its ear, leaving it to convulse and fall to the ground. As it reanimated, another bit and reinfected it, and Enzo tore out both their brain stems. Another grabbed me by the scruff of my neck, but Enzo bit his hand clean off. The fingers wiggled and the hand flopped to the ground while Enzo finished the zombie by splitting the top of its head, then tearing out its brain and part of its spinal cord.

One infected jumped on Alexander's back shaking the precious vial from his hand. With one swift movement,

Kane grasped the container, and his free clawed hand tore off the attacker from his progeny's back. In another quick movement, he slung the zombie into the whirling blades of the helicopter some fifty yards away. Its body was sliced into pieces and flew in every direction. Bloody pieces of flesh came splattering back. Kane, Alexander, James, Enzo, and I dodged the flying pieces while continuing to battle against the onslaught.

We battled our way to the waiting transport, and Kane managed to push Alexander into the passenger side of the aircraft.

As it lifted, a swarm of almost normal-looking humans surged out from the surrounding trees and threw their bodies at the windshield and doors and then lay on the landing skids. Many hung off the tail trying to pull it down. Kane began to rip their bodies in half and was soon surrounded.

As the helicopter began to lift, more emerged from the trees and held onto any part of the craft with a ledge. They resembled thousands of ticks attached to a bird. Kane slashed at them with clawed hands cutting them in half, but more pressed into him.

Zandra and her ten brothers flew into action with us, pulling and pulverizing the attackers. Zylon and Zeb alone tore bodies apart with their bare hands. Zandra clawed out jugular veins, and Enzo took many of them out by biting into the end of their spinal cords and ripping them out, rendering the zombies incapable of movement.

The last attacker went for James' arm and was met with a mouthful of metal.

Finally free of most of the hanging bodies, the helicopter sped into the air. Alexander opened the door and planted his steel-toe boot in the face of one of the zombies still attached to the skids, but the creature held on. The vampire soldier roared. Metal flashed. Alexander swiped alongside the helicopter so fast it looked like a part of the rotor blades. Body parts started falling from the sky. Each piece gave a wet splash when it hit the ground.

Alexander sent us all a mental picture of the ground littered with body parts of the infected. Arms, legs, heads, and torsos scattered across the open area between the house and vineyard. Black blood covered the ground, and the grass underneath it turned brown and then darkened to black. All of us but James were covered in dark blood.

Kane reached over and wiped a large piece of bloody pulp from my head, and I licked his hand. He then slapped a once-again spotless James on the back. *Impressive!*

I sniffed at my sire. *Did any of the zombies scratch or bite you?*

Not a chance. Kane smiled down at me.

I turned to James.

I am fine, Moon. No scratches or bites. James rubbed my ears while Kane looked me over to ensure I hadn't been harmed.

As we turned toward them, the other coven leaders applauded.

Zandra snorted, *Thanks for lending a hand... not.*

Leander spoke for all. *We knew you had it under control the entire time.*

Well done. Marco continued to applaud. *That's what I call skill and teamwork.*

The brothers slapped each other on the back as if they'd done all the vanquishing by themselves, and the coven leaders laughed.

Zandra ran to her husband, took him by the arm and me by the collar, and pulled us into the house. *Let's get inside. We might need to regroup somewhere else now that they know where we are.*

Kane laughed as we all entered the house. *My dear, they are controlled by Satan. He always knows where we are. If you are suggesting hiding, forget it. We will defend ourselves here until we have the formula to distribute.*

∞

Oddly, no further attacks ensued on us. Alexander reported having to patrol and fight off a meager few, but nothing he couldn't handle. Enzo, Kane, and I felt that Satan knew we had bested him on this one and had already moved on.

True to his word, Brogio's CEO friend delivered the potion to Alexander who flew it back to the estate. The coven members, Zandra, and her brothers, along with Kane and James, distributed it as planned.

We waited two days and then decided to head to Florence to assess the situation. Everyone would take bat form, leaving only the brothers and Enzo to guard the estate along with Brogio and Selene.

Before we left, Enzo approached me. *I don't want you to go.*

Why?

I can't be with you. He snorted. *I have much magic but don't have the ability to become a bat and fly.*

You need to protect the humans and the estate. I will be in flight and safe the entire time.

He shook his coat and placed his head over my neck. *I still don't like it.*

Before leaving, each of the vampire leaders dispatched their covens to various regions of Italy to survey and report back.

Since I had never morphed into a bat before, I followed Kane and Zandra's lead and began to run, visualizing the bat form in my mind. Soon I lifted off the ground as my bones cracked, popped, and compressed.

We flew in a colony, as bats do. My bat body felt weightless. Continuously flapping wings amazed me. I soared up above the camp of other insectivores and marveled at how connected we all felt even in this form. I had to imagine bats had the same connectivity as we had. Kane led the colony with echolocation calls, an ultrasonic sonar that bats use to navigate. The sound vibrated through my entire small bat body. Launching myself downward, I cruised through my bat-morphed progeny, weaving in and out and among them. The freedom of flying exhilarated me as much as the bloodlust or the thrill that ran through my body whenever Enzo looked at me.

As we travelled, we spied dozens of morgue trucks and ambulances cleaning up the dead body parts on the road into Florence. We swooped through the narrow streets of the city and then, as pre-arranged, split up to explore each area of it. Veering off from the others, I flew near the Hall of Five Hundred and spotted carabinier or police inspecting cars for permits to enter the historic section. As I wound my way through my assigned area of the most historical part of the city, I realized that people appeared to be carrying on in normal fashion. No one attacked others. Oddly, they behaved as if nothing had happened. I connected to Kane to share my observations. *Master, people are acting like normal humans. Two men are standing on the street corner laughing. A man and woman just greeted and hugged each other without anyone getting bitten. A small café near the Hall of Five Hundred is filled with people drinking and eating. It's as if they don't recollect what they have just experienced.*

Delight accompanied Kane's thought as it wove through my mind. *Yes. I know. I will explain later.*

In a darker part of the area I explored, I landed on the shoulder of a statue and listened as passersby carried on regular conversations. I perceived glimpses of their chatter as they walked past my perch.

"I think we should stop to eat. It's getting late."

"What time is the meeting at work tomorrow?"

"My new suit has blood stains on it. I can't figure out how that happened."

Once I had completed my observations, I headed home.

I landed on a giant oak tree between the house and the winery and hung upside down for a moment, just because I could. Flopping to the ground, I morphed into my hybrid-wolf body and gave myself a thorough shaking.

One by one, the others joined me.

Kane landed and began to transform, his bones still popping and cracking, as he walked to where I sat waiting. We were soon joined by Zandra, James, and the coven leaders.

My sire took in a sharp breath and let it out. It wasn't a sound that I'd heard from him often.

I've seen what each of you experienced. The infection has been eradicated. Those infected that had remained whole were restored, and none of the remaining humans appear to have been harmed.

Everyone nodded in agreement.

Leander placed a hand on his master's shoulder. *Our coven members—*

Have discovered the same throughout Italy. Kane completed his progeny's thoughts.

The door to the estate opened, and Brogio, Selene, Enzo, the brothers, and Snow Blood's wolf-pack family joined us.

Enzo strode to my side. *It is complete then.*

Yes, we all thought in unison.

I turned to Kane and stared up at him. Before I could ask, the question I intended was answered. *Yes. I included an ingredient to make them forget.*

But, I said as I nudged one of his knees with my nose, *why do they think they have dead body parts to clean up?*

He reached down and scratched my ears. *Before they can investigate, they will have forgotten. For those who have lost family members, they will have no recollection of them, nor will they question any abnormalities associated with it. It was the kindest way for me to prevent their pain and grief.*

I closed my eyes as Kane scratched my ears, but I still had concerns. *Won't people see pictures of their family, children, and wonder who they are?*

Yes. He removed his fingers from my ears and took Zandra's hand as she moved closer to him. *Through time and discussions with others, they will realize a significant event has taken friends and loved ones away from them. Because they will have no memory of them, it will be less painful. But they will start to investigate what happened, and that will be something we can deal with in the future. For now, we must focus on the survival of the entire planet.*

I stood in awe of him as did the others. He might have been viewed as a monster by some, but to us, except for the humans in our group, he was who we all aspired to be.

EPISODE FOUR

EVIL SEDUCTION, *AGAIN*

Enzo and I stretched out together on the cool marble tile of the front entry of the house after he had accompanied me for a hunt in the woods with James and Zandra's brothers. Snow Blood, Nova, and their pack had joined to chase us through the forest for a good hunt as well. They had always enjoyed tracking prey as our kind do.

Kane, Zandra, and the coven leaders had preferred to enjoy human nectar to break the fast the next night and enjoy the company of Brogio and Selene before they retired to bed.

As I lay snoozing, my paws jittered on the marble tile remembering my instinctive urge to run. I had felt joy as I had leapt over tree stumps, swerved around oak and maple trees, and scattered small creatures with my brothers and sister. We had all followed Snow Blood and Nova ahead of us. Chase, Thor, and Gaspar led us on a merry run, with Joker and Fergus on our back legs. Zandra's brothers had morphed into their wolf forms and howled ahead of us with my biological parents. James, transformed into a gray wolf, had run with them in a different direction.

I licked my chops and twitched my nose at the remembered taste of the blood of a mountain lion and a moose I had shared with my hybrid-wolf siblings while the brothers, Snow Blood and his pack, along with James took down a bear and another moose.

My pleasant thoughts were interrupted by Enzo growling.

I raised my head and eyed him, and he shook his head at me.

Another vision? I sprang up, now alert and full of dread.

Kane's voice sliced through our brains. *Enzo, Moon, join us. Tell us.*

The two of us sprinted back to the house and padded into the den, and everyone drew closer.

Enzo sat back on his haunches next to the fireplace, and I walked over to Kane's chair and sat.

Everyone's eyes focused on my spirit wolf.

My vision was garbled this time. Thousands of shards of glass being reconstituted into a frame. Satan presiding as if an orchestra leader. His laughter filled my brain with dread. The pieces of glass… or a mirror… falling back down on the ground as the fuzzy image of a Shadowhunter whirled around it all.

Lilith! Kane's word made my head pound. *Satan is trying to bring back Lilith!*

Brogio, his thoughts jumbled, stood abruptly. *Lilith? The original succubus?*

Yes, the mother of all evil. Zandra's eyes flashed as she conveyed the image of the redheaded temptress to us.

You told me she tried to possess you, control you, to spawn a demon. Brogio picked up his wine glass and went to the bar.

Yes. Kane joined his sire.

Brogio turned to his first blood son. *Magnum, a Shadowhunter, helped you trap and destroy her.*

Kane sipped his wine and watched his glass as he twirled it in his fingers. *I imagine Lucifer Morningstar has the power to put her back together again. God help us.*

∞

The hour grew late, just after two in the morning, and Brogio and Selene took Snow Blood's pack and wandered off to sleep.

I lounged on my bed next to the fire. Enzo sat staring at me from his cushion adjacent to mine.

Joseph startled me by jumping up and performing an impressive backflip, expertly missing Zandra's sleeping brothers spread out around the den floor. He ended his acrobatic feat by landing on the entry way. *What say we go for a run and hunt for prey since we missed it earlier?* He looked from Leander to Alexander and Marco, and then swung his green eyes around to Ian, Leslie, and Mia.

Alexander did a somersault over to Joseph and laughed out loud. *I'm up for it.*

The others strolled around the large hybrid vampire Lycans and over to them. They turned to look at Kane who was being thoroughly entertained by the amorous attention of his wife who sat in his lap.

Joseph rolled his eyes and snorted. Then, he turned to James who had just dressed in a silver shirt and pants with matching boots. If I hadn't known better, I'd think he'd taken up Kane's former dandy ways. The former servant shook his head and disappeared into the kitchen.

The brothers appeared oblivious and almost unconscious except for their loud snores. It was rare to see them sleep, so Joseph shrugged, and the coven leaders swept through the door and out into the night.

Enzo appeared impatient.

What bothers you, my friend?

Don't you think everyone is being a bit too unconcerned with the impending evil that could befall us at any moment? His eyes traveled to Kane and Zandra who paid us no mind.

I stood and stepped out of my plush maroon bed. *What would you have them do, Enzo? We have nowhere to really look for Lilith or Satan at this point. It would be unwise to try to find the devil in his own environment. If Lilith returns, then everyone will leap into action. Until we know what we are facing, what would you have us do?*

My spirit wolf sneezed and then walked to me. *If we were attacked, the coven leaders are in the woods. The brothers*—he tossed his head toward Zeb's sleeping form—*are out cold. And your master... well, he's preoccupied. What kind of preparation is that?*

I licked his face. *Have you ever known us not to rise to the occasion, even when surprised?*

He sat down and stared me in the eyes until his body froze as Selene's shouting brought everyone to their feet.

∞

Kane, Zandra, James, and all ten of the brothers were on the circular staircase before I could react. I hit the bottom of the stairs in three bounds, leaving Enzo frozen in place behind.

Kane had thrown open the door to Brogio and Selene's bedroom, and everyone ahead of me appeared to try and squeeze into the entrance at once.

"Something has him! It's sucking the life out of him!" Selene fought at the invisible force, trying to push her body between her husband and the entity that had him in its throes before it threw her off the four-poster bed.

This quickly brought back memories of Kane and Zandra in the same situation with Lilith.

Before anyone could move forward, both Snow Blood and Nova vaulted onto the bed, growling, snarling, and gnashing fangs into the faint outline of something attached to Brogio. My siblings and the wolf pack howled and took turns jumping on the bed and biting the air.

The coven leaders, covered in fresh blood from their hunt, rushed the door, pushed the hybrid brothers aside, and stared in amazement as Brogio's breathing became labored while he thrashed and fought at the slightly visible attacker.

Enzo wiggled into the room and flashed us all a vision of a naked woman with black wings and tail. Her red hair twisted around both her and her victim like snakes. The room grew cold as the entity sucked breath in a thin stream of fluidlike air from Brogio.

With that vision of his sire's attacker, Kane grabbed the creature by the throat and wrenched her off Brogio, breaking her connection to him. At that moment, James pulled the knife that he always carried from its sheath and jammed it with a powerful thrust into the demon's chest.

Its withering screams filled the room, and green smoke lingered where she had last been. The smoke turned to black ash and dropped to the tapestry rug covering the floor.

Brogio came up fighting, leaping to his feet on the bed. Blinking, he looked around the room at the multiple faces staring back at him. *What the hell happened?*

James grabbed a hand towel from the adjoining bathroom and wiped the green slime from his knife.

Kane eyed James and nodded. *Good man.*

Turning to Brogio, Kane held his hand out to his sire. *I believe you've just met Lilith.*

∞

This unsettling event sent the house into an uproar. Everyone gathered in the den around Kane who presided in front of the fireplace.

Satan has managed to bring the succubus back. He scratched his chin.

Brogio joined his side. Standing together, they were like dark and light, with Brogio's long silver hair and violet eyes and Kane's shoulder-length dark hair and almost-black eyes. Brogio stood only three inches taller than his first blood son. I mused at what a handsome pair they made. A small amusement to quell my distress.

Brogio turned to Kane. *My guess is that Lilith will be about creating other succubi to attack us.*

Zane boasted, *They won't be able to touch us.* He smiled at his brothers.

You are wrong, my friend. Kane shook his head. *When Lilith attacked me, I was nearly helpless. If it hadn't been for Moon, Zandra, and James at the time, I'd have been incapable of fighting back.*

Zylon scoffed out loud, *How can that be? We are strong, powerful. We have killed creatures more dangerous than a female spirit.*

Zandra went to her brother's side and took his arm. *Yes. You are powerful. But she is the ultimate female seductress. She was the original Eve who cheated with Satan on Adam in the Garden of Evil. All the children she spawned with Satan released evil into the world for the first time. She attacks men primarily and sucks out their souls. Once she attaches to you, she becomes irresistible.*

My wife is correct, Zylon. Kane ran his hands through his hair. *For a mortal man, she takes his will to resist away from him. I know from experience that only my preternatural abilities allowed me to hold off her power over me until the guardians who watch over my rest time stopped her.*

Brogio put an arm around his blood son. *He's right. As a human, I am now powerless against a creature such as she. Only my previous millennia as a vampire gave me the strength to fight and not succumb completely.*

Alexander marched to the bar. *I need a drink.*

Marco joined him, and then turned to Kane. *So, you said she's probably spawning more creatures like herself? How would she do it?*

I hopped up from my bed by the fireplace and went to stand by Zandra. *Like she did before. Sex with Satan.*

Yuck! Selene cringed.

But that would take too long, Leslie chimed in.

Kane walked to the bar, poured several glasses of wine, and brought them back to Brogio, Selene, and Zandra. *Everyone, please help yourselves.* He filled a glass for himself and walked back to the fireplace. *I've done extensive research on this in the past. Here's how she can do it. In addition to Satan's demon seed, she can reproduce using human semen from the human host she is possessing. The demon climbs up on the male organ and lies down on it like a dog or cat. She uses her organs to send intense signals of pleasure to the host and then produces ejaculation and takes the semen. The host is not completely conscious during this but is aware something is happening.*

That's disgusting, I interjected.

It's rape. Zandra sipped her wine.

Lilith and her kind were the first rapists. Kane stared into his glass of wine.

Mia repeated Leslie's earlier thought. *But being pregnant is a long process.*

Kane shook his head. *A succubus can produce a litter of new succubi in a matter of hours. One mating alone can spawn a litter of twenty offspring.*

I looked around the room at the shocked faces of our family.

Zane scratched an ear and ran his hand through his short, shaggy hair. The muscles in his arm rippled with the movement. All the brothers' massive muscles never ceased to amaze me. I could see his question formulating. *Don't they attack women?*

The male counterpart, an incubus, attacks females for the same purpose. Kane reached out and pushed a long strand of hair away from his wife's golden eyes.

Zale took a step forward. He clenched his strong jaw and asked through clenched teeth, *What's to stop her from creating those?*

We can only hope she doesn't. Zandra took her husband's hand. *She transformed herself into Kane's image and tried to seduce me. My guess is that she can be either succubus or incubus because of her status. If these creatures don't transform into one or the other of us, we'll probably be safe. Just don't be amorous with anyone until we get through this.* She laughed out loud and squeezed Kane's arm.

What happens to the host or victims of these things? Zachary rubbed his eyes in disbelief at what he'd just heard.

Kane sighed. *These creatures suck the life out of their victims. Their victims become lifeless husks.*

Ian put his arm around Leslie and pulled her close. His thoughts were forever about protecting his beloved wife. *So, you think she's going about impregnating herself with innocent humans in order to multiply an army and attack us?*

Not only that—Enzo rose from his fireside bed and padded next to me—*but each of her offspring does the same.*

Which means it's faster for the succubi to attack males and become impregnated as opposed to having incubus plant their demon seed in females. The succubi's incubation time is only hours compared to months for a human or canine female. James went to stand next to Zandra, his sire.

And, because female vampires can't conceive children, the female members of this family...

And Snow Blood, his pack and family, and me... Enzo added.

...will have to help protect the rest of us. James glanced at his sire.

All eyes fell on Selene, the now-human ex-vampire. *Oh, for God's sake. I'm on the pill.*

The house roared with laughter and then sobered quickly.

At that moment, Snow Blood, Nova, Chase, Thor, Gaspar, Joker, Fergus, their mates and offspring padded into the middle of the room. Zandra, Selene, Enzo, Mia, Leslie, and I joined them. Our thoughts mingled and became one. *We are ready.*

∞

The following night, the eighteen of us who were immune awaited the inevitable. We had eighteen vulnerable males to protect.

Zandra had enlisted Noble to secure combat knives. He returned with Ontario MK 3 blades used by the U.S. Navy Seals. Zandra and Selene oversaw Noble and his staff dipping them in a poison solution that Kane concocted the night before. They knew a blade to the heart or head wouldn't stop the succubi, but thought it gave them a fair chance at stopping them in a fight.

I would use my venom, and Enzo his supernatural abilities. Snow Blood, Nova and the wolves and their offspring would fight in a pack, and Leslie and Mia would double-team.

By sunset, Lilith and the offspring she had reproduced began to attack each of our vulnerable males. They hit us just before Kane and the vampire coven leaders rose from their rest.

Because we were all linked telepathically, I knew in an instant what was happening. Leslie and Mia awoke to Ian and Marco struggling and choking in the catacombs. Like cats from hell, they ripped at the two succubi attacking their loved ones. Ripping with claws and fangs at the translucent creatures, Leslie and Mia tore the two demons from their mates. In swift movements, the female coven leaders plunged the poisoned knives into them. The demons' unearthly screams shook the underground resting place and assaulted my ears.

The moment they vanished into green vapor, two more succubi took their places and pinned down Marco and Ian again. As Leslie and Mia fought the second attackers,

Alexander, Leander, and Joseph gasped for air as three more vile creatures attempted to suck them dry. Chase, Gaspar, Thor, Joker, Fergus, and their mates attacked them as a pack, dragging them off their intended victims and tearing out their semi-visible throats. Three more succubi replaced the fallen creatures. As the pack tore into them, the succubi lost control of their invisibility and made clear targets for the ferocious wolves.

Snow Blood, Selene, Nova, my sister, and four brothers watched over Brogio. Kane's recent research had revealed that shining a light into the face of the succubus would make her eyes visible. Once one of the succubi attached to Brogio, and Selene saw him struggling; she used a flashlight to illuminate its eyes. With that point of reference, Snow Blood and his pack covered the entity's body and ripped it to shreds. They continued to take on each subsequent attack as it came.

In our sleeping room, Zandra and I watched over Kane and James, along with Noble, who wasn't immune to attack. I had to fight the sleep-enforced rest that weighed on me but managed to shake it off when Zandra shook me. As Kane fought and gasped for breath, Zandra used a pin light to make the creature's eyes visible, and I tore at it with my fangs until I latched on to the side of a face and tore it out. Noble, who was trying to assist in pulling the creature off his master, was immediately attacked and pulled to the bedroom floor, while what felt like Lilith herself attached to my sire.

Zandra morphed into her black demon wolf, her golden eyes glowing. She jumped, wrapping her four legs around the creature's snakelike body that covered Kane. Wrestling Lilith to the floor, she wrapped her jaws around the succubus' throat, tearing at it. Its body dissolved into ashes.

At the same time, I bit into the back of the head of the creature trying to suck the life from Noble. The poor manservant's face became wizen and old as the creature pulled at him. Twisting around in anger, the thing tried to attach to me, and I lashed out at the source and felt a soft crunch as Lilith's offspring dissolved into smoke. As soon as the thing was gone, Noble recovered his youthful appearance. The next time he was attacked, he used his poisoned knife as I pulled the entity back from him, and it dissolved into ashes.

Because we were able to give Kane time to recover, he quickly morphed into a deadly demon, one I had never witnessed before. His appearance terrified me, and the rage I felt course through my blood was not mine. His head became triangular. Fangs protruded from wide jaws. Two glowing red eyes bulged from the side of each line of the triangle. Horns sprouted from the top of the triangle.

My head was filled with the sound of the buzzing of flies, and a putrid stink assaulted my sensitive nose. I felt dizzy and thought I might pass out.

His body shimmered and sprouted long arms with extended claws on each. Legs reformed into long and slender but deadly claws.

The next succubi to appear were immediately torn apart and consumed by the creature, increasing its vomitous smell.

Zandra, Noble, and I backed away, assured that this creature Kane had morphed into had no issue with handling its attackers.

Rushing downstairs to the brothers and James, we watched in amazement as Enzo, who solely guarded the hybrid vampire Lycans, protected them. Even though Zandra's brothers had the same ability to ward off their attackers as Kane did, my spirit wolf leapt from one succubus after the other attached to each of them. Not only did he bite off their heads but also ate part of them at a dizzying speed. I stood in the entryway with the automatic blackout curtains drawn down to protect me from the sun and marveled at Enzo. With his help, each of the brothers morphed into a demon as Kane had done and fought off several attempts to control them. Enzo did the same for James. Once Enzo yanked off a creature, James used his ever-present sword to cut them in half, rendering them to ashes. As soon as he vanquished one, another would attach to him. He struggled until Enzo freed him and then again turned his attacker to dust. I marveled at what a strong hybrid vampire James had become. Who would have known that the gray servant would become a silver knight?

The grip of fear that had taken hold of my body with the arrival of the succubi soon dissipated as they dissolved in defeat.

As everyone gathered together, weary from battle, Enzo froze again.

We waited in dread until he shook his heavy, shaggy black coat and his golden eyes gazed into mine. *I see her multiplying into the thousands. Thwarted by us, she will now attack the humans.*

∞

Not again. Brogio's thought resembled everyone else's. *Do you have a potion for protecting the humans against these creatures?*

No. Afraid not. Kane sighed and ran his hands through his hair.

Chase, Gaspar, Thor, Fergus, Joker, and their mates scratched at the door, and James let them in. Thor shot a thought to all, *The coven leaders and their progeny are safe in the catacombs.*

Yes, Kane smirked. *They have resumed their daylight slumber.* He stifled a yawn.

My biological sister, Novette, sauntered over to my sire. *Tell us the story of how the Shadowhunter helped you the last time, Uncle Kane. I love the stories you told us in the past about our father and our family.* She weaved her body in and out of his legs, and he reached down and rubbed her hybrid-wolf head.

Not now, sweetheart. I need to come up with a solution to this next problem. Kane's fingers absentmindedly tweaked her ears.

Wait, Brogio thought, *Novette is smart like her sister.*

I perked up and barked in agreement with the original vampire.

Can the Shadowhunter help us again? Brogio began to pace.

No. He told us not to call upon him again. Kane shook his head.

How did he help before? Novette continued to weave through Kane's legs. *And what is a Shadowhunter?*

At that moment, Noble and several of the black-clad, silent servants brought in sustenance in crystal glasses on silver trays to help all the nightwalkers fight off the need to sleep during the daylight and to give the rest sustenance and strength. Noble placed a bowl of my beloved O Neg in front of me. The wolf pack received generous portions of meat on platters, which the brothers eyed even as they drank their human blood. Brogio and Selene graciously drank the kale smoothies Noble had prepared for them.

Everyone savored the repast and then looked to Kane for the retelling of what some of us already knew.

Kane sat in one of the plush chairs near the fireplace and rubbed Novette's head as he directed the story to her.

Shadowhunters are also known as Nephilim. They're a secretive race of beings who are humans born with angel blood. They fight demons and have lived in a Shadow World for more than a thousand years. They've created their own civilization within human society. They are dedicated to keeping the peace in the Shadow World and hide it from everyday life while protecting the inhabitants of both worlds. Magnum is the name of the hunter who helped us with Lilith before.

Novette, as impatient as me, placed her nose under Kane's hand and flipped it onto her hind end as she twirled around to get a good butt scratch. *So, how did he help stop Lilith?*

She can't be killed but is fascinated by her own reflection and can be trapped inside a mirror. Magnum helped us trick her into an elaborate video mirror that projected my reflection from inside it. Because she wanted me, she became intrigued, and then he shoved her inside the mirror, and we broke it into hundreds of pieces.

And then she couldn't escape?

Exactly. I padded over to my sister. *Enough questions of my sire now, Novette.* I nosed her away from Kane and took her place as his hand rested on me.

Kane sighed. *We won't get help like that again.*

You are wrong about that, Kane. A voice from the entrance way startled us, and we all turned in its direction.

Magnum! Kane sprang from his chair.

∞

The deep voice startled me. I spun around to see the tall and slender, but muscular man with curly blond hair, angular cheekbones, and piercing blue eyes standing behind us. He wore formfitting black leather pants and a black tank top. His arms were tattooed with the symbols that Kane had described as runes the first time I had met him. He wore a military-style belt. A dagger hung from it.

How could he have surprised us in such a manner? Enzo shot his question out to us, and I felt his embarrassment at being taken by surprise.

One of his many talents includes his silent footsteps, I responded with pride at having knowledge that my all-knowing spirit guardian didn't.

Enzo turned and licked my face. *I know that Shadowhunters are mortal, but their angelic blood gives them special abilities to achieve beyond those of normal humans.*

Kane took two quick leaps and landed in front of his former enemy.

I telepathically let everyone in the room know about Magnum's former history with Kane. *In the 1900s, Magnum had believed my master was a dangerous demon and needed to be destroyed. They had fought, and my sire had bested him. But, because the Shadowhunter was vulnerable, Kane had spared his life to illustrate that he didn't have evil intentions. Because Magnum is a moral creature, he helped us with Lilith before as a way of payback, I think.*

Kane's gritted his teeth and crossed his arms. "The last time you were here, you threatened to kill all of us on sight when you encountered us again. Don't tell me you're here to complicate our already difficult existence."

Kane's face distorted. His fangs and claws dropped, and he took a lightning fast swipe at Magnum who amazingly dodged injury by folding backward like a man performing the limbo.

"Kane, stop!" Flipping backward and landing five feet away from my master, Magnum held out his hands, palms first.

Kane rushed to the Shadowhunter and grabbed him by the throat.

Magnum struggled as my master squeezed but pulled his dagger and took two sharp jabs at his attacker's tightened hand.

Agitation from my kindred slid through my body, and I warned, *Let this play out. The Shadowhunter may be here to help us. I sense it.*

Kane roared and flung Magnum into the wall. The Shadowhunter sprang up in an instant, hands held out in self-defense. "Kane, we are here to help. Not harm."

Kane halted in his tracks. "What?" Kane scratched his chin. "Why?"

"Because we must." Magnum stood staring at us one by one.

Reading his mind, we all saw a vision of a host of half-angel demon fighters, dressed like Magnum, standing outside in the courtyard. The bright sunlight shone down on them.

Zeb mumbled, "What the…"

Kane interjected, "You said you would never help us again, Magnum."

The Shadowhunter sighed. "That was a different time and circumstance. You are fighting for God now. We, even as earthly inhabitants, are part of God's angelic force. We are here to fight with you."

Zandra walked forward, and Magnum bristled at her nearness.

She smiled at her husband. *He thinks I am an abomination, that all hybrid vampire Lycans are unworthy to be near him.* Zandra stepped closer, goading the hunter to take a step back. "If you are going to fight with us, you'd better get rid of your high-and-mighty attitude, Shadowhunter."

"My apologies, Zandra. Old habits." He moved closer.

She grinned at him. "You and your brethren must be exhausted after travelling from the Silent City."

As if on cue, Noble stepped forward. "We will prepare food for your guests, sire." He turned to Magnum. "What do Nephilim eat, sir?"

Magnum threw back his head and laughed. "We are half-human, servant man. We can eat what humans do."

As Noble scurried off, Kane commanded him out loud, "Set up the tables outside in the courtyard for our numerous guests." My master then turned to me. "Come, Moon, it's time to succumb to our imposed rest." Taking Zandra's hand, we mounted the stairs. He turned back to

Magnum. "Enjoy the food. I'm told Noble is quite a good chef. Rest. Tonight, we will join you for supper after sunset."

Enzo and James followed us to guard outside our door until nightfall.

∞

As the sun set, we arose and found Brogio, Selene, and Zandra's brothers engaged in a pleasant conversation with Magnum.

Turning to his former enemy, Kane smiled and opened the door for the numerous hunters who had remained outdoors enjoying wine. "Please, come inside. Let me make introductions."

As Kane went about identifying our family to the Nephilim, Enzo turned to me. *It won't do for us to discuss strategy aloud with these new compatriots. Satan has invisible spies everywhere and…*

We will speak through telepathy then, Magnum interjected before Enzo could finish his thought. *Will the Father of all Vampires and his family be able to hear us?*

Yes. Brogio sauntered over and stood next to his first blood son. *Kane has made it so.*

Kane offered wine to our allies. As they all raised their glasses, he declared, *After a repast in the courtyard, we'll discuss strategy.*

∞

Kane sat scratching his chin as Magnum finished laying out a plan to once again rid the world of Lilith and her ilk.

I pressed against my master's left leg and placed my chin on his knee. *If this plays out the way Magnum suggests, Enzo and I should accompany them.*

Jubal, one of Magnum's compatriots, leaned in with his elbows on the table toward Kane. Long tendrils of black hair hung in mocking eyes. Much taller than Magnum, he hunched over the table. He smirked as he spoke. *Is it normal for your kindred pet and her wolf companion to go with you most of the time?* The Nephilim's tone and body language conveyed a lack of respect for what he considered a lower species. He seemed less kind and more egotistical than the other Nephilim.

Kane flashed a row of white teeth, with only slightly elongated incisors. *More like all the time.*

Then, I agree with the hybrid's suggestion. Jubal gave Magnum a sidelong glance.

Kane gritted his teeth. *Her name is Moon Blood. He is Enzo. You have been introduced.*

Forgive him, Kane. My master's long-time frenemy glared at Jubal. *And the rest of them for that matter.* He looked around the rows of outdoor tables. *They know very little about your true history and only consider the rumors. What they should understand is that you now fight with us against evil for God. Once they see Moon and Enzo in battle, they'll change their tune.*

They don't have to wait. Kane sent an image of Enzo and me in battle to all present. It showed me running through berserkers and biting off large chunks of their legs as I went. Once bitten, the flesh eaters would fall to the ground with their bodies shaking and foam pouring from their mouths before they stopped breathing. Following that image, Kane sent another of Enzo scampering over the enemy, unhinging his jaw and biting off their heads.

Jubal whistled out loud. *Impressive.*

Zeb and his brothers stood abruptly. Zandra's oldest sibling stared down at Magnum. *If we're going to do this, we'd better get started. We've only got a good six hours before the first rays of light appear. The nightwalkers among us won't do well if they're caught by the sun.*

I stood up and barked as thousands of bats fluttered from the trees and disappeared, like a throng of insects, down the entrance hole into the catacombs below the estate. They soon rose and scattered for their nightly hunt.

Kane turned to Leander. *They should remain in their chiropter form safe in the dark here so as not to be attacked by the succubi.*

Yes. Leander smiled at his friend and leader. *They have already been instructed to do so. They know to take refuge in the catacombs from the light in our absence when it is time.*

The coven leaders, James, Brogio, Selene and their pack, and Enzo gathered around Kane, Zandra, and me. Zandra's brothers stood to the side waiting for instructions.

We should be safe until sunrise, which will give us time to get to Paris. Kane stood with his hands on his hips in deep thought. *I have another wine estate outside of Paris where those of us who need to hide from the sun can do so.* He looked at Magnum. *Do you and your fellow Shadowhunters need transportation to meet us in Paris?*

You worry about your family. I'll take care of mine. Magnum raised an eyebrow at his old enemy.

Wait. I looked around at everyone. *Why does my family need to go to Paris?*

Kane stroked my head. *Because Lilith will expect us to be here.*

We have just one loose end. Zandra turned to Magnum. *What if Lilith and her demons try to attack our men in Paris?*

Each of us has already selected one of you to duplicate. We will remain here in your place during the daylight hours. As I have explained, we are not vulnerable to them because of our angelic blood. Lilith and her succubi will waste the early morning at sunrise trying to figure out how "you" have figured out how to resist them. Magnum grinned, his eyes twinkling at his own cleverness.

But, if you stay here all day, how can you get to Versailles in time? I padded forward and looked up at Magnum who smiled down at me.

Not all of us need to stay here and impersonate your family. There are enough of us to spread around. Magnum chuckled at his comment.

So, when you come to our hideout in Paris, you will already be disguised as my family? I looked to Kane and then back to the Shadowhunter.

Kane placed his hand on my head. *Yes, Moon, but you will know the difference. Lilith most likely won't. We can only hope that Satan is too absorbed with making succubi and planning his next move to see through our ruse. His ego often clouds his ability and allows us to pull off deception as well as he does. Your biggest challenge will be overcoming the forced sleep that nightwalkers must endure. But you have done so before.*

∞

I felt the hand shake me awake. I struggled up through the drug-like sleep that the daylight forced upon me. Kane lay in a dead-like rest with Zandra's left arm and leg wrapped over the top of him. We had arrived at Kane's wine estate in Reims, just outside of Paris, as the sky first streaked with faint pinks and purples. I must have fallen into my rest for all of five minutes since a sunrise departure had been planned.

Turning, I saw my master standing before me.

I shook off the sleep as I stood up on the bed.

It's time for us to go, Moon. I recognized Magnum's voice and thought how amazingly like Kane he appeared.

He read my mind and smiled. *Yes, and all your family have been duplicated as well. Follow me.*

A line of limos with blacked-out windows sat waiting in the estate's underground garage. Zandra's imitation brothers required three separate cars due to their bulk. The rest of us took up the remainder of the other three vehicles. Enzo and I climbed into the lead car with my master's look-alike.

"Let's move it," Magnum called to the driver. "It's already a quarter past six."

The cars whisked us away to our destination upon his command.

I sat up next to the Kane imitator. *Won't the Hall of Mirrors be filled with tourists?*

Not at seven in the morning. It isn't open to visitors until nine, so that gives us a couple of hours to make this happen.

I didn't bother to ask what we'd do if Lilith didn't show up or how he could attract them away from my family. That hadn't been clearly explained, even though I knew all the females were with our males to protect them as they had before. So, I turned my attention to details about the building we would soon reach. *What is the Hall of Mirrors exactly?*

The Zandra impersonator seemed amused, and when he responded, I recognized his voice as Jubal's. *It's a massive room that measures 240 feet long and 34 feet wide. It has a 40-foot ceiling.*

And lots of mirrors, I guessed.

Jubal disguised as Zandra smirked. *The principal feature of this hall is the seventeen mirror-clad arches that reflect the seventeen arcaded windows that overlook the gardens. Each arch contāins twenty-one mirrors with a total complement of 357 used in the decoration of the galerie des glace.*

I see. Since Kane and Magnum had used a mirror to trap Lilith before, it made sense that 357 mirrors could trap her and her offspring demons. But I still didn't know how it was going to work, even though Magnum had discussed it with us earlier. The Nephilim had held the finer details close to his chest indicating that we should trust him and the other

Shadowhunters. Kane appeared to do so, but I had my doubts.

The cars entered the Palace grounds through a service entrance, which I had to imagine Magnum had arranged. Stopping at the back of the ornate Palace of Versailles, the impersonators, Enzo, and I followed the disguised Magnum through a covered portico and a series of hidden doors.

The Shadowhunter stopped in the darkness of a doorway leading to what had to be the Hall of Mirrors. *This is as far as you go, Moon.*

I could see why. Daylight entered the space through 17 immense windows that illuminated the plentiful gold leaves and the multitude of sculptures and paintings. Facing the windows, huge mirrors were comprised of the 357 smaller panes that Jubal had described. Each mirror across from a window made up 21 panes, as best I could tell. I looked up at the Kane imposter. *If I couldn't enter, then why bring me here? Why not just have one of your people impersonate me?*

He looked down at me. *For your smell, dear girl. Lilith can smell your vampire blood. You give the aroma that will attract her and her minions to us.*

Indignant, I sat down hard on that one. *I don't smell.*

But you do to a demon. Stay here.

My family's imposters walked out into the morning sun of the room. I thought Kane would have loved to feel the sun on his face. I thought the same. Then I sat up straight with another thought. *You're not asleep, and you are standing in sunlight. Lilith is going to know this is a trick.*

Let's give her some more incentive. Magnum marched toward me, pulling the blade from his belt. *We need your blood to draw her to us.*

Enzo growled and skidded in place next to me before I could blink. He bared his teeth and growled.

The Kane imposter held out his hand. *No harm intended. But each of us needs a drop of your girl's blood here as a draw for the succubi.*

I licked Enzo's face. *It's all right.* I held up my left leg, and the Nephilim cut into my vein. Each imposter came over and dabbed some of it on their necks, right at the jugular. Once finished, I licked the wound to stop the bleeding, and it healed in a few minutes.

Enzo busied himself by continuously licking the now closed wound.

All the imposters took their places in front of the giant mirrors. Their reflections in the morning sun were blinding.

I heard the screeching banshee-like cries of the neophyte succubi before they entered the hall, almost seeming to seep from the ornate gold leaf décor of it. They swirled around each of my family member look-alikes. The intense light made their outlines slightly visible. Red-, blonde-, and black-haired creatures writhed in the air. Black wings and long pointed tails lashed out at the Nephilim imposters. Fascinated by the mirrors and their own reflections beside the imposters, they reached out and gently touched the reflections of both their faces and those of the impersonators. I sat up in shock as their fingers appeared to seep into the mirrors.

Screeching that sounded like an oncoming locomotive combined with the rumble of thunder permeated throughout the hall. A flash of red swirled around the succubi, and Lilith's voice, like fingernails on a blackboard, cried out, "Don't be fooled, sisters! This is a trap! They've tried this before on me, but I'm free once again." Her laughter bounced around the room and caused me to cringe.

In unison, the demons each attached themselves to the Nephilim as Lilith floated above like an orchestra conductor. To the succubus' surprise, her offspring were instantly thrown off. Each spat out the obvious bitterness of angel's life force that they'd drawn in.

They backed away but quickly attacked again, this time pulling out breath. Their eyes turned white, their skin began to wrinkle, and once again they retreated. Their cries of frustration rang in my sensitive ears. They had no power over the Nephilim.

Magnum disguised as Kane pulled a dagger, spun into the air, and plunged it into Lilith's heart. She swirled, screamed, and transformed into the most wretched hag I'd ever witnessed. Her skin wrinkled and darkened almost to black. Her red hair peppered with white streaks. Her chin grew to a point, and warts popped up on the end of it. Her hands and feet became talons. Her black wings and long pointed tail appeared to be razor sharp.

Swirling about she touched each of her young offspring who instantly became haggard crones with elongated claws on their hands and feet. Their tails became daggers, and they rushed the disguised Nephilim, trying to slash them into pieces.

They wounded several of the Nephilim who crawled to the corners of the room to try and recover. They bled profusely, but Enzo leaped to each and began to lick and magically heal them. He had the same healing tongue that my master possessed. As he worked, several succubi attempted to attach to him, but he swirled and, with one bite of his unhinged jaws, took off their heads.

Jubal, who now appeared as Zandra, drew a glowing sword and began to methodically sever the heads of multiple succubi. The other Nephilim followed suit. Heads were lopped off and rolled along the shining floor of the hall.

Lilith flew, screaming. She crashed into Magnum, and the two of them slid across the polished floor. As they did, Magnum reached around to a sling he wore on one shoulder and pulled out a gilded, glassine chalice the size of an ordinary wineglass.

Flipping over, he grabbed Lilith's face and pressed the chalice against it. Lifting her with one arm, he ran with her as she fought to escape, but her efforts were futile. The chalice held her captive. He shoved her into a mirror. With that, each of the other imposters grabbed a remaining succubus and flung them into surrounding mirrors.

The screeching wails of the succubi assaulted my ears, and I flattened them in pain.

Enzo left our wounded Nephilim and ran into the shadows behind me and sprinted toward Magnum/Kane who was pulling a long duffle bag.

Magnum/Kane swooped down and pulled out a giant silver sword shaped like one from the Middle Ages my sire had hanging on his den walls. This one had a straight double-edged blade and a one-handed hilt. It resembled the Mortal Sword we had seen when we had gone to the Nephilim's underground city. Kane had said the hilt was made of pure adamas. He had explained that the ancient Greek word meant "indestructible" and was most probably where the modern word "diamond" had its roots. My sire had said adamas was linked to a uniquely strong and undefeatable quality. The hilt had an elaborate design of outspread wings emerging from the point where the blade met the handle.

The Nephilim disguised as my master swung the sword into the mirror in front of him and then ran smashing it into the mirrors that entrapped the succubi. They shattered into hundreds of pieces, and the banshee-like screeching of the succubi filled the room and sent a chill up my spine.

There. Magnum's voice filled my brain. *That should hold Lilith and her offspring for a while.*

∞

We sat in a den almost identical to the one in our home after the sun had set in Paris. My family consumed generous glasses of wine and had me retell the story of how the Nephilim had ended the succubi more than once.

But I don't understand the significance of the cup and the sword in all of this. Zachary, the logical Moretti brother, always had to have a thorough explanation, and Kane, the historian, was happy to oblige with input from Magnum.

The Mortal Cup, Kane explained, *provided protection for the Nephilim and gave them some authority over the demons.*

Ironically enough, Magnum offered, *the Infernal Cup was forged in 2007, but instead of angel blood that molded our Mortal Cup, Lilith's blood was used to create a demonic counterpart.*

And, Zachary questioned, *this Mortal Cup gave you some sway over the succubi, you say?*

Exactly. The angel Raziel gave the Mortal Cup to Jonathan Shadowhunter, the first of our kind. It is one of our most important instruments.

And the sword?

Magnum sighed. *It's agony to bear. Its weight and coldness give the holder a tingling sensation. It felt as if hooks embed my palms.* He held out his hands that still shook from his encounter with it. *Its main use is to compel the truth from its holder through pain. It metaphorically pulls the truth out of someone. Today, because it can be used for both good and evil, I was able to use the succubi's own demonic power against them. The cup held them. Satan can't overcome its angel-driven power. And the sword entrapped them.*

But, Zachary pushed for further information, *why did you choose to do this act in the sunlight? Wouldn't vampires standing in bright light have been a red flag for Lilith and her kind?*

Kane interjected, *We needed a smoke screen of sorts. Our duplicates remained here pretending to sleep during the daylight, when these creatures normally attacked us. The Nephilim needed time to get to the Hall of Mirrors while the succubi were distracted. The demons, of course, were unable to penetrate the disguised sleeping imposters. Their frustration became unbearable to them. It was the only timing that would work. Having Moon's blood to draw them to the Hall of Mirrors, while the creatures were already confused, and the smell of her blood put them in a frenzy.*

Zachary raised an eyebrow. *These creatures could smell Moon's blood from all those miles away? Why weren't they drawn to Kane instead?*

Magnum smiled. *They can smell active blood from anywhere. That's why we opened one of Moon's veins and smeared our throats with her blood. The fresh blood on our necks overpowered that in Kane's or the other hybrids' veins.*

I nudged Kane's knee. *Why did you and Magnum keep so much of your plans secret from the rest of us? We knew only the bare details.*

Because, Moon, Magnum said as he leaned toward me, *Satan often seems to know and hear everything we do unless we are especially deceptive. Kane projected a blocking spell when we were discussing it earlier with all of you. We had to make sure that the devil couldn't read anyone else's thoughts but especially ours, so keeping everyone in the dark meant Satan couldn't detect our actual plan.*

Joseph, trying to interject some levity, remarked, *It is a good thing you didn't get caught or leave any fingerprints behind. I'd hate to have to foot the bill for all those broken mirrors.*

Kane and Magnum simultaneously let out a groan.

On that note, Magnum rose from his chair and walked to Kane, who stood to take the Shadowhunter's outstretched hand. *We must return home now, Kane. But we will be watching and available to help when you need us.*

Kane looked deeply into the Shadowhunter's eyes. *No words can ever thank you and your brothers and sisters enough, Magnum.*

With no other words, the brood of Nephilim exited the front entrance and disappeared.

Everyone stared after them, and Joseph expressed all our thoughts. *Those are some amazing allies.*

EPISODE FIVE

DING-DONG, THE WITCH IS (FINALLY) DEAD

Father, I beg you. Kane sat with Brogio, Selene, and Zandra while Enzo and I lounged by the door. The coven leaders, James, and the brothers, along with Snow Blood and his pack, had opted to hunt for prey in the surrounding woods on Kane's French wine estate while the rest of us enjoyed human blood.

No, son. We won't leave you in this time of great need. Brogio savored one of Kane's fine Bordeaux.

Zandra reached out and touched Selene's arm as they sat together on a small sofa. *Think of your son, Adam. You've been gone for a while now, and I worry Satan might try to harm you through the child in some way. The kindred protectors that are watching over him might not be enough. Why not take more coven members and go home to make sure he is safe?*

Selene sat up, and her eyes somehow pleaded while demanding her husband listen to Zandra's words. *She's right.*

Kane stood and began to pace. *You were a tremendous help when we were attacked before and then had the zombie infection with which to deal. But this latest attack by Lilith left you so exposed. I don't think I can deal with anything happening to you, Selene, or Snow Blood and his pack. The best way you can help is to keep Adam safe right now. This is a battle I have been chosen to fight. Like it or not. Please stop putting yourself and the rest of your family in harm's way. Go home to Wolfville. I can't be at my best with all of you to consider. The coven leaders will gladly send many of their progeny to meet you there and provide protection.*

Brogio stood, drained his glass, and sighed. *All right.* He looked at his wife and then Zandra. *You are right. We need to make sure Adam remains secure from all of this.*

Kane stepped to his blood sire's side and slapped him on the back. *I've already instructed my coven leaders to send two hundred of their best progeny to meet you at your estate. They are already on their way.*

Selene and I will leave tonight.

Zandra stood with Selene, and they hugged. *I'll have Noble send your things from Tuscany to you.*

Brogio and Kane scurried off to the study to make airfare reservations on a red-eye.

I heard Kane making his blood sire promise to call if he needed anything. *And call me if you have any troubles in Nova Scotia with any of this mess.*

∞

As the moon rose over the Chianti Hills in Tuscany, I rose with an unusual hunger.

Enzo met me at the sleeping-room door. *James wants to hunt in the forest for breakfast. Are you game?*

I wagged my tail and headed down the stairs where James waited, naked, his white hair in a knot at the base of his neck.

He opened the door, and the three of us, eager to go on the prowl, sprinted out into the glorious night. Remaining in our true forms, we dashed around cypress and cedar trees, leapt over fallen logs, and smashed loose rocks with the strength of our feet.

I stopped suddenly as I picked up the scent of two rutting moose and then led my companions straight to the mating animals. It was sad to end them just as they conceived new life that would never have the joy of living. But then, the cycle of life is cruel and holds no guarantees, especially with hungry vampires on the hunt.

I took the male down while James slaughtered the female. Each of us latched on to their jugulars and emptied them of their life blood in a matter of minutes.

Enzo stood back behind me, and I didn't notice his frozen stare until I had been sated. Sitting back and licking the last droplets of blood from my mouth and jaws, I realized he was in the throes of a vision.

When his eyes focused, I walked to him. *You've had another warning.*

Yes, and you aren't going to like it.

I never like any of your visions, even though I am very appreciative of them. What did you see?

James finished his repast and joined us.

Before Enzo could convey his vision to us, a foul-smelling green fog rolled in and around us.

I raised my nose to the air and took in the rotten odor mingled with the smell of fresh mist as it covered us. A heavy dampness fell over the three of us, and I knew none of us were able to push it away or take more than a few steps. I fought to move forward, but my legs refused to properly obey me.

Our lush woods swirled with mist that thickened, and the hair around my neck tingled.

Out of the mist ahead, three blurred, smoky images of a single woman moved in unison. The images simultaneously cast out their arms, as if inciting a spell.

I moved like a sleepwalker in a dream to Enzo's side, touching his face with my nose. He felt like stone! I turned and snarled at the images, but the heavy weight of the mist held me back.

The three forms moved slowly toward us. Once in front of me, they solidified into one woman. She wore a black sleeveless gown that seemed to ripple as if the cloth was ink spilling off her. Her black robes displayed ornate silver designs like the alchemy symbols Kane had once showed me in one of his books.

Her black hair was pulled into an ancient Greek-style, high-set ponytail. She carried two old-fashioned reed torches and a wild-looking cat. She put down the gray-striped Maine coon–like creature, and it weaved in and out of her flowing robes and hissed continuously at us.

A deathly pale marred the woman's beauty. Her presence engulfed the woods around us with a strong condensation of the mist. A green aura shimmered, surrounding her. I could feel magic swirling around me.

I glanced at James and Enzo who appeared immobile and stonelike. I bared my fangs, saliva dripping from them, and lunged at this mythical sorceress. But nothing happened. I couldn't move and felt blocked, almost paralyzed, when I tried to step forward.

"So, you are Moon Blood, one of the whelps of Snow Blood…" Her voice was deep and raspy. The green mist swirled up and down her body and her dark-black eyes shone like coal in her pale face. "He was once mine you know, until your filthy kind stole him from me."

I looked at Enzo and whined.

"They aren't dead… yet. I've waited too long to take my revenge on your kind for locking me away."

I sniffed the air around her. She smelled like cold death and moist earth. The faintest hint of oily tar hung around her. The shock of who she was hit me like lightning. Kane had told us the story long ago of how Hecate, goddess of witches, had kidnapped my biological sire and tried to make him her familiar. She was the evil entity who had tried to ensnare Seth after he had fallen to Earth. But Snow Blood and Selene convinced Hades to reduce her to tar and trap her in his domain forever as revenge for her murdering my biological sire's beloved second-in-command, Scrawny!

As I stood looking at this hated creature, Kane's story of her demise flashed through my mind. My sire's voice filled my head.

Snow Blood and Selene followed Hades to a mirrored opening where Hecate lay in a puddle of oil, her skin cracked, and she sobbed and begged for mercy. Hades left it to Snow Blood to continue her suffering or not. Snow Blood wished for her to give up her life and immortality to stop her agony. She did. Black oil poured off her and seeped into the ground, and she surrendered and melted slowly into a black puddle into the Underworld. Hades explained she had always wanted to return to the Underworld and rule it. She had fought him for that right, and he was glad to destroy her. He declared she would exist as the oil underneath the ground there for eternity. And, thus, Scrawny's death was avenged. Yet, Snow Blood had never recovered from the loss of his friend and companion. Snow had always held his friendship with Scrawny in his heart. He loved his second-in-command just a bit more than all the rest, except Nova. Perhaps because the gray wolf's love and loyalty had been so hard-fought before winning them.

Somehow, through his sheer magic, Enzo's thoughts filled my mind…

My vision revealed Satan coercing Hades to release Hecate!

…only to be interrupted by Kane's words. *I am coming…*

…and then the witch's words. "He won't make it in time because you will all die now!"

She raised her hand seemingly to strike us all down with her magic, only to be thwarted by the white light of an angel. It covered her, turning from white to gray and remolded itself into the form of a gigantic but slender wolf. Its silver wings spread out and covered the witch. Green gas mingled with white fog. They rolled as the witch fought at her old victim. Growls emerged from the outline of the wolf. Hecate's cackling screams made my ears ring. She tried to pull away, only to be sucked back into the body of the wolf form. They clashed and tumbled. Hecate rose above the wolf for a moment and shot a long bolt of black oil at him. It hit his light and fell to the ground with a thud like a bowling ball hitting a concrete wall. The wolf's light forcefully enveloped her, absorbing her, squeezing the life and magic from her until she dissolved into a black puddle of nothingness. In her place, a gray wolf stood. The kindness in his golden eyes melted my heart as I felt my body and that of my companions released.

SCRAWNY! Kane's strong voice filled my mind, and James and I whirled to see him standing behind me.

I watched as my sire approached the wolf who met him halfway. The angel wolf looked up at my sire and closed his eyes at the touch of Kane's hand.

How? Kane knelt next to the wolf, who now shimmered with white light that surrounded them both.

I could only compare Scrawny's kind, deep voice to music. *Upon my death, God the Father granted me angel's grace. You will understand soon how we were all a part of His plan for what you are now experiencing. I am just another tool to help aid you in your fight for Him.*

Kane ran his hands over the wolf's shaggy coat. *If only Snow Blood could be here to see you, to see what you have become...*

Scrawny's light began to fade. *I'm afraid, though, that I wasn't supposed to use my grace to take revenge on my murderer. That's how it will be viewed. But I saw no other way to save my beloved sire's child but to take out Hecate. She planned to kill Moon and her companions and then come for the rest of you. If I've broken a rule, I don't care. It was worth it to save this noble creature*—he turned to me—*her brave companions, and all of you.*

I walked to the angel that had been my sire's great friend and licked his face. My tongue tingled as it touched his fur, which became effervescent. *Thank you for saving and protecting us.*

As he began to fade, his voice lingered in my head. *Tell Snow Blood that I love him and that I will be waiting for him on the other side.*

∞

Zandra met us as we walked back toward the villa. She grabbed and inspected me and ran her hands over Enzo and touched James' arm.

We walked in silence for a while.

You know, Kane's thought broke the quiet walk, *only angel power could have defeated Hecate.*

Yes, Enzo agreed. *I saw Satan raise her from beneath the Underworld and infuse her with his own brand of angel power.*

Sometimes I feel as if we are just pawns to draw out Satan's attacks on us. Kane walked faster with that thought.

Zandra sped up and walked backward staring at her husband. *You know, I think you might have something there.*

I snorted out a sneeze. *I wish Snow Blood could have witnessed his beloved Scrawny's final revenge.*

Kane touched my head with his fingertips. *Never fear. I have sent him a vision of all that you experienced. His heart is warmed to know that Scrawny has received grace and that he is watching over us all, but particularly you.*

EPISODE SIX

THE FINAL BATTLE

The moon huntress Artemis locked arms with her twin brother Apollo, god of the sun. They were joined by Zeus, king of the gods and their father, his brother Poseidon, god of the seas, and Hades, god of the Underworld. The goddess, who had been nothing but pain and suffering for Brogio, Snow Blood, and my sire Kane, marched with evil intent toward me. My brain ordered my legs to move, but they ignored me.

How can this be? The archangels destroyed them.

Their eyes glowed and focused on me. Thin beams of light shot from them. As the light hit me, I howled in agony.

I sprang to my feet, dazed. Looking around, I slowly recognized our resting room at home. Kane remained asleep, but Zandra sat up and touched my hind leg. *Are you all right, girl?*

The dream… just now. It was so real. I even felt pain.

Zandra crawled around to my side and put her arm around my neck. *Tell me.*

I sat back on my haunches. *The gods and Artemis, the goddess. They were alive and coming for me. But they are dead.*

Not as of an hour ago, Enzo, who guarded us just outside our door, injected his thought for all to hear.

Kane sat up. *Makes sense. If Lucifer Morningstar can raise the undead, Lilith, and Hecate, he can bring them back too.* He bounded from the bed, pulled Zandra with him, and scurried out the bedroom door as the sun dipped and smoldered into the horizon.

I jumped down, and James, Enzo, and Noble met me at the door. We followed Kane's lead into the den, but Enzo paused mid-stairs, frozen in a vision.

After several minutes, he bounced down the stairs and scooted to a stop in front of Kane. *Satan is sending an army of undead in front of the gods.*

Just the skeletons? James questioned as he pulled his sword from its scabbard and another from a hall closet.

No. Zombies too, Enzo growled, and the hair stood on end around his neck. *The infected kind. Only now they're three times their normal size.*

The floor began to shake to the time of massive heavy footfalls. The crystal glasses on the bar shelves began to sing and clatter together, soon falling to the floor. The entire villa rattled.

Alexander, Leander, and Marco crashed through the door. *An entire army of undead is upon us.* Mia, Leslie, Joseph, and Ian crowded through the doorway. The scream of thousands of bats assaulted the air.

Zandra's ten brothers took to the stairs from above. Most of them were half-transformed into their werewolf bodies. Zylon bounded from the railing onto the marble entryway, morphing as he swooshed through the air, and landing with a loud thud on the floor.

Kane and Zandra rushed outside with the others.

I felt my body transforming into my inner demon.

Enzo flew out the door, sped ahead, leading the others. He sprinted across the vineyards, which were being crushed by thousands of 18-foot giant zombies. Some thousand nimble skeletons carrying silver swords led the assault in front of them. My spirit wolf suddenly grew to over ten feet tall and six feet wide and smashed into about twenty of the skeletons who tried to slash him into pieces with their deadly swords. He became a blur as he somersaulted over their heads, tearing them off and spitting them out at the speed of sound.

I stood in awe of him for a moment until I noticed thousands of bats swarming up into the nighttime sky. A tenth of them veered off, rose up high, arced, and pointed downward en masse. Just before the point of contact, they transformed into their human-vampire forms and, with their powerful clawlike hands, ripped off the heads of at least a thousand undead giants.

I flew with vampire speed attacking the giant legs of the undead and injecting my venom. As they shook and convulsed to the ground, James and Zandra followed me and tore off their heads and ripped out their hearts to prevent them from reanimating.

Zandra had morphed into a gigantic black wolf with yellow snakelike eyes. Long, jagged claws extended from her large paws. Her fierce fangs dripped with enemy blood.

James had opted to become an enormous red-eyed silver panther. His massive claws and fanged jaws decimated zombie after zombie.

Kane and his coven leaders took to the air, transforming into dragons.

As Kane's bones snapped and popped, I paused. I saw him sprout what looked like fifty heads from his shoulders and feathers over his entire body. His wings must have spread forty feet. Instead of legs, huge snake coils formed the lower half of his trunk. I had never seen him become so grotesque or so large.

Fire shot from his eyes and pinpointed the heads of undead giants. The fire spread to their enormous bodies as they swirled in agony and fell to the ground, shaking the earth and crushing smaller enemies in their wake. Fire raged around us.

I continued my surge on zombie legs, dodging being grabbed, bitten, or smacked. But I heard Kane's command.

Alexander, Leander, and Marco, join me as a Typhon dragon. Ian, Leslie, and Mia, we need three cockatrices. You will have the ability to kill by just breathing or touching the enemy. Joseph, we need a Chinese dragon. You can vomit the equivalent of a lake or an ocean on these monsters if need be. But hold off and circle. We may need you to put out fires.

The coven leaders paused, hovering in the air. Alexander shot his amazement to all, *He commands us like a true general.*

Surrounded by dead giant zombie parts, I chanced to look up as Alexander, Leander, and Marco transformed as Kane had. Ian, Leslie, and Mia each became two-legged dragons with a rooster's head. Joseph's body was covered in green scales, and when he opened his mouth, water grotesquely dripped from his wide tongue.

With the combined two hundred heads of Kane, Leander, Marco, and Alexander, they began to decimate the zombies by fire.

James, Zandra, and I dodged the flames as we headed toward Enzo and the werewolf brothers who were devouring bones faster than I could blink. Zandra and James joined them, challenging the skeletons only until Zeb and his brothers, who were now gigantic demon werewolves, smashed them with their powerful jaws. Grown to some fifteen feet tall, the brothers had become terrifying versions of any normal werewolf. Long black fur covered their faces and dropped to beards that dangled on their large muscled chests. Glowing red eyes peered out with deadly intent. Fangs jutted outward slashing through the enemy. They rose on their two hind legs and ripped and smashed through the skeleton creatures. Bones rained down left and right as they plowed through them.

I dodged around the skeletons and continued to take out zombies with my venom. Zandra joined me as I took them down with my poison while she ended their ability to reanimate by either ripping out their hearts or tearing off their heads.

Mia, Leslie, and Ian flew over the top of hundreds of zombies and merely breathed gray smoke on them, instantly killing them.

The vampire bats continued to reform, dive, and transform just in time to behead the numerous giants.

The Typhons obliterated the zombies by fire, while Joseph, the Chinese water dragon, spewed water on the vineyards to keep the fire from spreading.

I ran blindly from one giant leg to the next until none were left. I skidded to a stop with Zandra and Enzo behind me. As far as the eye could see, the bodies and bones of our enemies burned.

Kane circled above and gave the command, *Now, Joseph. Put out all the flames.*

All of us moved back and watched as he flew over the battlefield like a giant water bomber used to extinguish wildfires.

Once the fires were reduced to smoldering embers, Kane and his other coven leaders landed some fifty yards from us as I listened to the popping and snapping of the brothers' bones reforming behind me. I felt my own body shrink and reform with some discomfort.

After Joseph put out the extensive blaze, he landed in an area large enough to contain his size. We all watched in amazement as Kane and the coven leaders' bodies shrank, heads retracted, wings and snake coils became arms and legs, and feathers and scales became skin.

I had seen this many times before, but it was a sight that never ceased to shock me.

∞

Enzo nudged me as I watched the strong, muscular bodies of my sire and his kindred approach us. *This was just a prelude. Artemis, Zeus, Apollo, Poseidon, and Hades approach.*

The weariness of his warning seeped through to my very bones.

I watched as they marched toward us from the horizon, just as they had in my dream. I licked Enzo's face and then moved to my master who stood facing them, along with his wife, James, his coven leaders, and Zandra's brothers.

I pushed my head under his left hand and pressed my body to his naked leg. *This is where we will all end. We are not capable of destroying them. They turned you, Brogio, and Selene to cinders the last time you faced them.*

His fingers stroked my head, and he put his arm around Zandra.

Enzo pressed against my side. *I will end you myself and take your spirit to the universe with me before I let them destroy you.*

Kane tweaked my ears. *But we will die fighting.*

The unfurling of wings behind us was accompanied by a familiar voice. *Or, perhaps, we will even the playing field.*

∞

I whirled around as did my companions.

The white light of Seth and Mathias hovering just above the ground with three other abnormally large angels blinded me.

I recognized the archangels Michael, Gabriel, and Raphael from Kane's stories and images of the time they destroyed the mythological gods before.

Seth... what? Kane stepped forward.

Satan has taken unfair advantage by endowing his attackers with his dark grace. Seth shimmered as he spoke to us through his thoughts.

He isn't playing by the rules. The archangel Michael pointed to the approaching gods. *At every turn, he has cheated in some way.*

Rules? There are rules? Kane scratched his chin.

Raphael, the divine healer of physical ailments, stretched out his arm. *If Lucifer can cheat with dark grace. We can do so with heavenly grace.* His light extended in an arc to Kane, and my master was bathed in it. The white light expanded and covered each of us.

The glow of it filled me with joy. James fell to his knees. Black tears turning clear streaked his handsome face. Gradually, everyone knelt, heads bowed. The overwhelming sense of power surged through all of us. I could feel it growing.

As it settled within us, Gabriel motioned for us to rise. *You have just been empowered with angel grace. You are more than capable of matching these ridiculous gods and their egos.*

But, be forewarned, said Michael as he leaned forward toward us, *this is only temporary. Once the battle is done, grace will be removed from all of you.*

But how will we... Zandra started.

Use the grace? Seth finished her question.

Mathias snorted and stomped. *Think it, and it shall happen.*

With the sound of wings unfurling, the angels disappeared.

∞

Kane whirled around to face the oncoming enemy.

Their brilliance blinded us almost as much as that of the angels. Artemis' silvery light clung to her like mist to water. It lingered near her body, like it wanted to touch her but couldn't. Her twin, Apollo, threw off golden light that tempted to intertwine with hers but didn't. They were both beautiful, but their looks were tempered by a deadly strength that sent chills through me. Zeus' white curls blew in the swirl of wind and thunder that surrounded him. Like his twin children, his demeanor terrified me. Poseidon appeared much like his brother Zeus, except he carried a trident. Hades kept a slight distance from them. More than seven feet tall, his body was shrouded in a long black robe. He hovered above the ground, and I could see only his yellow eyes, black beard, and pale hands and feet.

Zeus held out his hands, and thunder cracked around him. A small ball of lightning formed in his palms, and he manipulated it as it grew to a larger mass the size of a football. It became a bolt of lightning. He placed it in one hand and pitched it with tremendous force toward Kane. Thunder roared from the heavens.

Kane shot a command to all of us, *Destroy it!*

Focusing on it, a beam of silver light shot from all our eyes and exploded the bolt before it could hit Kane.

Artemis pulled a silver arrow from the quiver on her back and aimed it at Zandra, while Apollo fired off shards of light carrying the sun's brilliance meant to burn me.

Zandra aimed her stare at the goddess, and her mind screamed with one word: *Melt.*

The arrow liquefied in midair and splattered the ground.

At the same time, I dodged Apollo's shards with faster speed than I had ever possessed as a mere vampire. I caught the shards with my mind and redirected them back to Apollo in a boomerang effect. The god was so surprised by my action that his own light knocked him to the ground. He growled as he rebounded to a standing position.

Hades shot fire from his eyes and tried to blanket us all with flames. Joseph, perhaps because he had been a water dragon, spewed water from his throat and doused the fire before it could touch us.

All five of the gods paused in surprise at our actions until Zeus marched forward and began to blow a great wind upon us. The force of his breath knocked us all back. We tumbled head over heels. The strength of his wind hit us like a hurricane, picking up debris and pelting us with rocks and dirt. Sand filled my eyes and blinded my vision. The moment Zeus took a breath, we struggled to right ourselves and stand. My family and I forced ourselves to balance against his assault.

As if on cue, the five of them combined their forces, raining down the power of silver and gold light from the moon and sun, lightning, thunder, and wind, and devastating fire and water that would have normally destroyed us.

We withstood unscathed by collectively projecting white light that encased us in safety like a bubble. The word *shield* came to all of us at once, and we acted upon it with our minds.

The gods looked to each other and sprang upward. Apollo, the god of light, brought forth the brilliance of the sun. Artemis joined him in the air, raining down the power of the moon. Zeus jumped above them and poured lightning in every direction. Poseidon opened his mouth and dumped a stream of saltwater over all of us. Hades alternated raining fire on us as well.

The powerful brilliance of the sun, moon, and lightning consumed the sky and the earth around us. We remained shielded and motionless, letting the gods exhaust themselves with their fury. Before the onslaught, Kane had tried to protect us all by spreading his arms wide, and Enzo leapt closer to me, trying to shield me, but the force of the gods' attack paralyzed us and only allowed us to shield ourselves.

Chaos reigned. Relentless fire, lightning, and painful light alternated with waves of saltwater raining down upon our shield. I thought this fire and brimstone would destroy our protection, and I anticipated being transported to Hades' Underworld or Satan's hell. We were subjected to this for what seemed an eternity.

They threw everything they had at us. Our collective muscles and strength screamed in agony. The heat of the fire and lightning burned our bodies, even with our shield holding. The earth rumbled beneath our feet and rocked back and forth like a quake trying to shake our footing. I kept my eyes squeezed shut to guard against the painful light. The wind screeched in my ears like a train engine bearing down on us.

We felt ourselves weakening momentarily but fought back and persisted on and on and held our shield against them. I knew that had it not been for the grace the archangels had given us, we would have all been long destroyed.

My mind raced with what we could do to obliterate them.

And Kane's thoughtful, ever-creative solution came to all of us. *Harness the power that the archangels used to destroy these gods when they attacked Brogio, Selene, Snow Blood, and me.*

But what...? Zeb and his brothers, most of those with us, didn't understand what had happened. I only knew from Kane's stories to my siblings and me. He shot a clear visual image of what he had experienced before. This time, Kane's reimaging was like a video replay:

When Brogio, Selene, Snow Blood, and I

last faced these monsters, they were ready to

destroy us when Mathias shot through the light,

streaking down like a bolt from the sky, his hooves

reaching out straight for Hades. The winged horse knocked Hades to the ground. Seth, all in white, followed with his wings spanning ten feet in both directions. He landed as softly as a leaf in fall before Artemis, and she stepped back. Three breathtakingly handsome winged men landed in front of the remaining mythological gods, who all moved back.

Seth's voice came out as a force of nature. "Let me introduce you to Michael, Raphael, and Gabriel."

They each bowed as they were introduced—Michael in front of Zeus, Raphael facing Apollo, Gabriel facing Poseidon. "If you would like to meet the other archangels, Ariel, Azrael, Chamuel, Haniel, Jeremiel, Jophiel, Metatron, Raguel, Raziel, Sandalphon, and

Zadkiel will be pleased to make your acquaintance." The threat carried weight.

Zeus tried to walk around an immovable Michael. As he tried to pass, Michael's body appeared to widen and expand. Zeus looked into Michael's face and took a step backward.

Michael is God's warrior. I flashed that thought to my kindred. Zeus would have no chance against him.

"Why would the archangels of heaven care about the destiny of these unworthy, vile creatures?" Zeus shouted out.

"Because," Seth responded, "they, like you, are God's creatures."

"What do you MEAN? We are the gods of the heavens, the earth, the seas, the sky, the moon, and the Underworld!" Zeus spat out, and lightning struck a nearby tree, destroying it.

Apollo tried to join Zeus' side, but Gabriel blocked him.

Dina, Hades' werewolf spy, leapt, jaws wide, fangs bared, at Brogio. Gabriel shot white light and instantly pulverized the creature.

Hades' face registered shock.

"You are all subject to God the Father's will." Seth's voice conveyed his passion for his creator. "He has granted his protection to Brogio and his family. You will leave here now and never approach them again. God has commanded."

Hades tried to put his hands on Mathias and fell to the ground in agony.

Artemis whirled, attempting to spread her silver light, only to have it shrink around her when it touched Seth.

Raphael and Gabriel pointed to Apollo and Poseidon, and both gods fell to their knees, their faces washed with agony.

Zeus attempted to throw a lightning bolt, and Michael caught it in one hand and threw it back at Zeus, flattening him to the ground.

Their final reign of terror on my kindred and me all but destroyed our physical being.

Through it all, Seth, Mathias, and the archangels stood steadfast. After the gods had exhausted their punishment, the heavenly soldiers rose in unison and circled around them. They spread their wings, and a light brighter than anything I had ever witnessed, except for God's, shot from all their eyes, surrounding Zeus, Hades, Poseidon, Apollo, and Artemis. The screeching sound that emanated from their power brought Snow Blood and his pack to the ground in excruciating agony. The gods who had made our

lives miserable for so long appeared to fade and

then implode. Silence followed.

    Afterward, the angels restored our

destroyed bodies.

Kane's imagery had the desired effect.

This is what we must do. Zandra linked hands with Kane and Zeb. Kane took me by the collar, and Enzo pressed against me. James took Zachary's hand, and each of the remaining brothers and coven leaders locked fingers.

We waited until the gods had exhausted themselves and released our shield and rose above them in a circle. An excruciatingly bright light shot from all our eyes as we merely thought the words *Let there be light.* The screeching sound that emanated from us along with the chorus of sound that rang from the heavens almost deafened me.

Zeus, Hades, Poseidon, Apollo, and Artemis writhed in agony and were forced to their knees. We continued for what seemed to be an equal eternity to the wrath they had brought down on us. The outline of their bodies began to shimmer and dim. Their screams of pain mingled with what sounded like a trumpet blasting from above. Their eyes bulged, and their heads expanded, and then, they imploded.

The air around us was sucked into the implosion, and all of us dropped to the ground in utter exhaustion.

Seth's gentle voice swirled through all our minds. *It is over. This was your last battle. You are victorious. Satan and his demons will trouble you no more.*

I felt the grace slip away from my body, mingle with that of my family, and ascend in white light toward heaven.

I closed my eyes and pressed closer to Enzo. Kane reached out and took Zandra's hand and my paw in each of his hands, and the world went dark.

∞

"A wager?" Kane screamed aloud, and his voice bounced off the walls as he stood staring at Enzo who had just provided some shocking information.

I padded over to my spirit wolf and stared at him.

Kane began to pace back and forth, sprinted to the bar, poured himself a shot of whiskey, which he downed in one gulp, and threw the glass into the fireplace. He whirled around and screamed his rage.

Why are you yelling? Zandra hopped down the stair, fresh from her bath, wearing jeans and a blue blouse and blue sneakers.

Kane swirled around to her and half-yelled, "You're not going to believe this! And go ahead and talk out loud. We aren't hiding from anyone anymore."

I sat back on my haunches and hoped my master would calm down.

"Okay, what am I not going to believe?" She skipped over to her husband and placed a quick kiss on his cheek.

Not mollified, he raised his voice. "Everyone, get in here!"

Seconds ticked by until Zandra's brothers strolled through the front door, wiping their latest meal from their faces. James followed and shut the door. Noble snuck in from the kitchen and stood in the corner.

What's happening? Alexander reopened the door and entered along with the other coven leaders.

Kane ran his hands through his long hair and snapped back. "Speak aloud. No reason to be secretive anymore. Especially since we're all just pawns at the whim of the Almighty and His fallen son!"

"What?" Zandra grabbed his arm. "Sit down, calm down, and tell us what's got you so upset." She walked to the bar and poured him a large glass of wine. She handed it to him as he sat down in one of the overstuffed chairs next to the fireplace.

Everyone gathered closer to him.

He glared at Enzo. "You tell them."

Enzo sauntered around to his bed next to the fire. *Well, I can't speak aloud.*

Kane drained his glass and threw it into the fire. "Don't be a smart ass."

Enzo sneezed and took a moment to lick his paw.

Zylon grew impatient and walked to the bar for the pitcher of fresh blood Noble had placed on it earlier. He poured a glass and gulped it down. The other brothers followed, and Noble rushed off to get more pitchers of our life-saving nectar.

I licked my chops but waited for Enzo to enlighten us.

Sitting back on his haunches, Enzo looked around the room. *Apparently, the battles we have been experiencing were the result of a wager between God the Father and Satan. If all of you could overcome everything Satan threw at you, then he would give up his quest to overthrow the Almighty.*

"A bet? A freakin' bet?" Zandra joined her husband's indignation.

Everyone in the room began to speak at once. I wanted to slink away and hide.

A wager, yes, but if you had failed then Satan would have ruled. Enzo stretched his front legs out and slid down.

How do you know this, Enzo? I walked to him and looked into his golden eyes.

Another vision.

"I don't understand." Zachary turned from the bar and cut through his brothers' raised voices. "Why couldn't God just have the angels battle the demons? Why us?"

"My question, exactly." Kane stood, and his eyes went from brown to red. He raised his arm to the ceiling. "He must consider us dispensable… didn't want to put his angels at risk. If not that, why us!" The volume of his voice increased as he spoke.

Without warning, my master's body was surrounded by the purist white light I'd ever witnessed. Rather than blinding me, it comforted me.

Why not you? Why not all of you? Are you all not the instrument of unconditional love for each other? Have you not given all to protect Earth and humanity and each other? When given the choice, to fight for ME, did you refuse? No. What more could I ask of my servants? Selfless acts of courage… that is what you are and always have been. Not evil monsters. You have done everything to live in peace away from others and sought not to use humans as food. You have only harmed others when they threatened you.

You are more benevolent than I intended when I created your breed.

All of us stood in shock at God the Father's declaration.

Kane's eyes widened. "What do you mean? Apollo, Artemis, and Hades created Brogio."

The white light swirled and settled. *I manipulated the demigods and engineered the first vampire so that he would create a warrior nation of vampires. Unfortunately, Brogio was gentle of soul and heart and refused to turn others into his own likeness to produce the army I needed. He hid in the shadows. Even when he became an enraged slasher after his wife's mortal death, he made sure to tear out his victim's hearts to ensure they wouldn't reanimate. So, I had him create you, Kane. I knew you wouldn't be able to control your bloodlust and would create bloodsucking rippers who would force Brogio to create an army to defeat them.*

We all stood paralyzed.

Kane shook his head. "But you gave Brogio and his family mortality."

The light softened around Kane. *Yes. A reward for playing his part.*

The light expanded and surrounded all of us. *Kane, I grant you and all those you love, all in this room, and all associated with them outside of it, everlasting peace, love, and prosperity.*

The light slowly faded, and I felt the utter joy of His embrace. It made all our troubles less important. We had all been touched by God the Father. We had been blessed for what we had suffered.

Kane swayed, and Zandra threw herself in his arms. "You have been given what you have always desired."

A huge cheer filled the room, and Zandra's brothers intermingled with the coven leaders and James, slapping each other on the backs and hugging.

Kane looked at his wife and murmured, "Yes, now that everyone I love is safe"—his eyes fell on me as well—"we can exist in peace."

EPILOGUE

As my family's celebration went on through the night, Enzo and I walked out to watch the bats flying in unison through the air. Apparently released by their leaders, they had returned from this last battle in Italy to their lives. I felt relief knowing that Brogio, Selene, Adam, and my wolf clan were all safe back in Nova Scotia.

I sighed and gave Enzo a sidelong glance. *You are my spirit wolf, but I love you. I love you like Zandra adores Kane. I can serve my master until the end of time, but I want more. I want you to be with me through eternity, and not just as my protector. Don't I deserve your love?*

Enzo placed his neck over mine. *Moon, you must know that I've always loved you, from the moment you were born as a hybrid wolf and then again when you became a vampire. When God the Father brought me the vision about the wager, I asked him to grant me a reward as well. He agreed. He didn't need to grant me eternal life. I already have that. He created me as a spirit to protect you. I asked Him to grant me the ability to be your mate, in every way.* He licked my face, and my dead heart came alive bursting with joy for a few seconds.

I knew that I would gladly suffer everything we had experienced again if it would end in this way.

My spirit wolf's golden eyes filled with love as he gazed at me, and my life was now complete.

Enzo and I raised our heads and howled out our joy at the full moon above.

And we all existed happily ever after… for eternity.

THE END

Dear Reader,

So ends the adventures of Kane and his beloved Moon Blood.

But be on the lookout for more adventures starring James, along with Brogio and Selene's son, Adam.

You didn't think they were just secondary characters, did you? Take Adam for instance. You don't think there's something magical about a child born of former vampires?

You will find a new narrator and hybrid vampire spirit wolf named Reign to love, too. Can you guess his origin?

And what about the ten Moretti brothers? How will they figure into these continuing adventures?

Wait and see... or sign up for my newsletter at

Unconditionally,

Carol

Thank you for reading Moon Blood: The First Blood Son (Book 5). Reviews are a tremendous help for authors. If you enjoyed this book, please leave a review! Even a few words would be a huge boon.

Want to know when the next installment comes out? Join the exclusive readers group for GIVEAWAYS, Advanced reader opportunities, prizes and Pre-order notifications!

Go to:
http://www.carolmckibben.com/free-ebook.html

Next Book in the series:

REIGN: The Assault of Lucifer Morningstar

About Carol McKibben

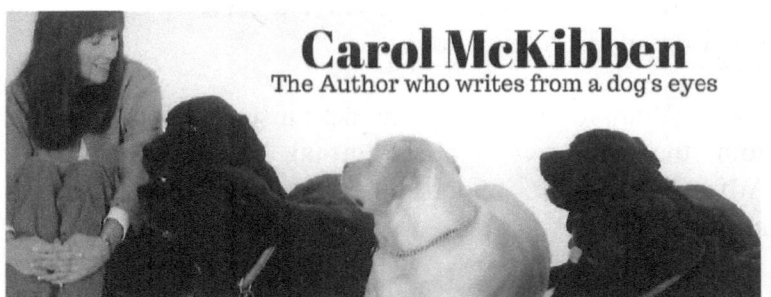

Carol McKibben
The Author who writes from a dog's eyes

Carol's love of animals, especially dogs and horses, is obvious in everything she writes. When Carol isn't feeding her horde of canine rescues, she's out riding her beloved Friesian on the plains of Texas. Her love of animals leads her to write through a dog's eyes. Carol's message is clear. "If a dog can love us unconditionally, why can't we do the same with each other?" And, her paranormal stories are often filled with characters that might be the most difficult to love.

Carol's writing career began at 14 years of age when she started telling her stories to Labrador Retrievers, Basset Hounds, and any stray that happened by. It wasn't long before people stopped to have a listen as well. Now, Carol writes for people and speaks to large audiences, dogs included.

Connect with Carol McKibben:

Facebook:

https://www.facebook.com/CarolMckibbenAuthor

Twitter:

https://twitter.com/CarolMcKibben

Goodreads:

https://www.goodreads.com/author/show/4046806.Carol_McKibben

Bookbub:

https://www.bookbub.com/authors/carol-mckibben

Website:

http://www.carolmckibben.com/

Want to be notified when Carol has a new release on Amazon?

1. Go to: http://www.amazon.com/Carol-McKibben/e/B00B6HDRVU
2. You'll be taken to Carol's author page where you can click the "Follow" icon for her new release notifications.
3. You're all set!

We often update our books when grammar errors are found, so please let us know if you've found one at: stephanie@trollriverpub.com

Find Other Great Books from Troll River Publications

www.trollriverpub.com